The Lotus of the Dragon

Betsey Grobecker

The Lotus of the Dragon

Printed in the United States of America

Preface

My adult walk on this Earth has been a journey into the deepest depths of my beingness to unveil the wisdom and magic that life's deepest essence is. I was gifted with highly evolved spiritual mentors from different traditions and countries. My work with them was a journey of releasing false truths about myself, and western science, by allowing a grace that is untouched by worldly energies. It is a grace that pulsated through my beingness, creating space for my soul to sing Its song through my physical form.

What follows is a work of fiction that mirrors my own mythic journey through its characters. I took great liberties in presenting mythic figures in the image they embody to me, which often contradicts current personas. For example, I presented the goddess Kali in the image of a possible future potential within her that I gave life to in this story. The characters do not seek to be validated or invalidated as a standard of truth. They simply seek their expression through this story for you to relate to as you wish.

How the characters know life is quite different than how western science knows life. I was a researcher specializing in Learning, Cognition, and Development. At the same time, I was venturing inward, searching for a wisdom I believed was absent from the science I was taught. Answering the call of my heart, I left my academic career to unveil my inner chalice of wisdom. What was revealed is not what western science accepts as truth, but it is my personal truth.

Allow your imagination to soar as you relate to the characters. Do not think your way into truth through your mind and intellect. They are limited without the support of grace and cannot reveal the wisdom that life is. Feel into your heart to know your own truth and always stay true to that.

Acknowledgment of Spiritual Mentors

B elow is a short list of significant spiritual mentors whose energies most impacted this novel. They are presented in their order of appearance in my life.

The Late *Jyoti Chrystal:* A shaman who introduced me to the feminine wisdom that transcends creation's male and female polarities. I first experienced a blending with nature's consciousness in my work with her.

Joseph Rael: Although I never met him on this physical plane, his shamanic energies deeply impacted me in Native American ceremonies that included Sun Moon Dances led by his students. In his books, I learned about the sacred medicine wheel that is of creation's dual spiraling energies. The medicine wheel is consistent with the work of physicist David Bohm, who spoke of the unfolding and enfolding of energy from the Holomovement, or totality of All-that-is. All forms, or relatively autonomous sub-totalities of movement (i.e., fields and particles), are abstracted from this totality of All-that-is.

don Agustin Rivas Vasquez: An artist and ayahuasquero in the Amazon area of Peru. His guidance over a four-year period when I lived in his jungle camp for four to six months at a time, opened my heart to blend with the spirit of Mother Ayahuasca and her wisdom. Her spirit inspired my dragon's creation as the union of the serpent and eagle energies, and how I spoke of nature.

Yug Purush Mahamandaleshwar Swami Paramanand Giriji Maharaj: An enlightened spiritual Guru and philosopher in India. I lived in his ashrams for over six years, writing books in English on his teachings. My heart expanded into beautiful light, but the harsh spiritual practices and living conditions in his ashrams weighed my heart down into density. Significant teachings touched upon were: the three states of the mind's awareness and the Awareness that transcends the mind; the gunas or "knots" of the heart that are ignorance, desire, and action; and the sheaths of the personality.

Tobias and Adamus Saint Germain: Unembodied Sovereign Creators and Masters, whose essences are channeled through Geoffrey Hoppe, and assisted through Linda Hoppe of the Crimson Circle. Significant teachings touched upon were the sovereign One, creation's story, Adam and Isis, and the darkness of our divinity.

Mikael: An unembodied Sovereign Creator and Master whose energies blend with Robert Theiss of Ancient Wings to give voice to his teachings. Working deeply with Mikael for the past five years, his essence deeply impacted this story. Significant teachings touched upon were: creation's story; the sacred triangle of the sovereign One that is the human self, Intuitive Self, and Eternal Self; Archangel Michael laying down his sword; and the three A's of Acknowledge and Accept the thoughts of the mind, and Allow the grace of the soul to transmute them.

One

I was born a little over 12 years ago in a small village in west central India. Nani Mishka, my maternal grandmother, suggested I be named Aditi, which meant creativity, freedom, safety, and abundance. Aditi was the "Mother of Gods". Liking what this name meant, my parents readily accepted Nani's suggestion. Nani wanted me to have this name because she knew the potentials I could realize in this lifetime. She also knew the potency these potentials carried, which could bring great challenges to all of us. Nani thought it best to keep quiet about possible challenges ahead.

I was told my sister, Pari, who was two years older than me, always wandered into the room I was in. Now older, we continued to enjoy each other's company. We were often busy assisting my mother with daily chores. I always found play in my chores and seldom minded them. Early this morning, as I sat with my mother and sister by the river washing clothes, the rising sun reflected its light upon the water as twinkling stars. They danced with joy for the experience of another day as their sparkles disappeared and reappeared in the river's current. Feeling the rhythm of its dance beat within my body, I scrubbed and rinsed the clothes to the rhythm of the water's flow. I loved being with nature. It always offered me its magical play when I gave my attention to its beauty.

Himmat, my brother, was a year younger than me. He did not have time for housework and was free of it. Himmat went to school six hours each day, while Pari and I attended school only four hours each day. There was limited money to pay for teachers, and educating boys took priority over educating girls. Unlike Pari who was chatty and sociable, Himmat and I had a solitary nature. Himmat was very studious and did well in school, but Pari and I thought he was far too serious about his schoolwork.

My favorite activity at school was archery. We lived on the outskirts of a forest, and dangerous animals such as lions, sometimes wandered close to the village. Many times, if people planned to wander outside of the village, they took an archery set with them in case an animal came too close. The animals seemed to sense danger. For the most part they stayed away, even though our village and others continually invaded their habitat as our populations grew.

Nani Mishka also lived with us. No one could have a more perfect Nani. Most women in my village Nani's age looked much older than her. Their bodies were heavy for their height as if they needed the extra weight to support the sadness I saw in their eyes. I never saw the playful twinkle of Nani's eyes in their eyes. Nani's body was of medium height and weight, but her weight seemed to magically transform itself. At times, her body was a feather that was too light to stay on the ground. At other times, her body was heavy with a strength that could not be pushed to the ground if a force attempted to do so. I witnessed the playful twinkle of Nani's dark, almond-shaped eyes transform into a piercing gaze that could stop a bulldozer in its path.

At the edge of our property, there was a small house where Auntie Kiara lived. Auntie was my mother's younger sister by about five years. Her house was just out of sight from the large home my family shared as if wishing to be hidden from view. Auntie never married and had children. She seldom left the house and its surrounding grounds. I was puzzled why she was not like the other women who had a husband and children, and why she never ventured into the village to buy things she needed.

But I loved Auntie and accepted things as they were. Auntie's presence made me think of her as one of the goddesses in the temple. I could not decide which goddess she was because there was a quality of every goddess that I felt in her. Most times, I did favor the goddess Kali because Auntie wore her extraordinarily dark skin. At times, I believed I saw Auntie's skin turn a deep navy blue, just as I sometimes witnessed in Kali's statue. Nani said Kali's blackness, and her swollen belly, expressed the darkness of creation's great womb that creates and destroys. Auntie's body was not as large and full as Kali's body, but I felt her strength in Auntie when her very dark, almost pure, black eyes peered into my eyes.

My classmates were afraid of the goddess Kali. Her

physical appearance easily created fear in the most fearless of minds. In our village temple, Kali was a passionately black figure with four arms. She held a sword in her upper left hand, and a bloody human head slain by her sword in her hand below it. I learned at school that Kali's sword represented the higher spiritual knowledge, attained by severing the head of our human ego to overcome the cycle of birth and death. I was unsure what that meant, but I understood there was darkness within me that I had to conquer. Her right hands extended out in blessings to those who worshiped her. A garland of human heads was worn around Kali's neck and the upper part of her swollen belly, and her bloody tongue stuck out. One of her feet stood upon her husband, Lord Shiva.

Violence always showed itself in stories about Kali. We were told she is our protector and should not fear her. I did not fear her, but most of my friends stayed a good distance from her because they did fear her. In a mighty battle, Kali killed the demons who represented the dark forces of the world. Through her raw, untamed warrior energy, Kali celebrated her victory by dancing over the corpses of the demons she slayed. The intensity of her thunderous dance grew and could not be tamed. When it threatened the collapse of the world, Lord Shiva placed his body under Kali's thundering feet. Although in a trance, Kali became aware of Shiva's body beneath her and slowly came out of her trance to end her wild dance.

This morning, my class went to the temple to see a play a younger class was putting on about Lord Shiva. I was enjoying the play, especially the singing. But I was also distracted and annoyed with some students who were giggling about a boy who could not carry the tune. I sometimes witnessed the statue of the goddess Kali glow with light as it assumed life-like qualities. Today, she wanted to play by showing me a lotus in one of her right hands. The lotus had both light and dark throughout it.

Looking at the others, I knew I was the only one who saw Kali's lotus. Teased by her play, I felt the darkness of the lotus within my heart. It was a feeling of deep love and acceptance for everyone, just as they were. My annoyance with those who were giggling left me. As I shared a smile full of joy with the boy who could not carry the tune, he looked far less nervous. His singing improved as tension left his face. I would have to talk to Auntie and Nani to see if they could help me understand what happened during the play.

Auntie Kiara's house was an exceptionally special place where I could talk about anything, even the nature spirits and light beings I continued to see. When I was about six years old, I agreed to acknowledge these beings only when at Auntie's house. The light in her house held the warmth of the sun's radiance that pleased the beings who hung out there. Auntie's house was small and simple, but in my heart, it was an eloquent castle filled with a light that other houses did not have. I painted and wrote about the nature spirits and light beings my heart saw only at Auntie's house. I was so alive in joy there. Sometimes I thought I would explode if I did not paint to express my joy.

As the sun lost its intense heat to the late afternoon, I finished the last of my chores. Finally, I could go to Auntie's house. Most likely, Nani would also be there. Almost every day, the three of us shared chai and biscuits in the late afternoon. Nani and Auntie won my love and trust simply by their joyful presence. Even the worst problems of a 12-year-old melted into nothingness when they spoke to me. Their words were full of a beauty I did not feel in the words of other adults.

I ran to Auntie's house. The momentum of my run was absorbed into the door, banging against the wall as I opened it. Hearing my hasty entrance, Nani and Auntie stopped painting. Nani loved to go to Auntie's house to paint when she had free time. Auntie sewed six days a week for my father's customers at his cloth shop. She was up very early in the morning to have her sewing done by lunchtime. She wanted afternoons and early evenings free to paint.

Nani went for water to clean the brushes, and Auntie went to the kitchen to make chai. My enjoyment of smelling the chai spices as they simmered always made me a willing helper. Today, I was anxious to share the events about the play, and I poured the chai before the spices were fully infused into the water. Finally, we made our way to Auntie's small table. They barely sat down before I began to talk about the play.

Auntie's grin on her face widened as I shared the event. "The goddess Kali shared her lotus with you to bring your attention out of your mind's emotions and into your divine heart to feel its joy. You enjoyed Kali's compassionate love before, and you readily let go of your annoyance to experience it once again."

Auntie stopped the dance with her words for Nani to

continue this dance with her words. I barely noticed the change of voices. There was a rhythm between Auntie and Nani in everything they did. I never witnessed two humans communicate with such ease. It was a dance of light within the crystals of a magical ballroom filled with the sun's rays flooding through its huge windows. The movements of one partner melded with the other, then flawlessly separated as playful light occupied the space their parting bodies created.

"Kali reveals her wisdom in such playful ways. The bloom of the lotus rises from its roots, which are embedded in dark mud. Our inner heart is the bloom of the lotus, but the darkness of our wounded human heart hides the lotus bloom within our divine heart. Painful memories become a dark, dense veil covering its joyful radiance. This boy's father is critical of his voice. When the boy attempts to sing, he feels the pain of his father's words and cannot carry the tune. As he allowed your compassion to lighten his heart, he forgot his fear of singing poorly. The compassion you both experienced is the grace of the lotus."

"Before I saw the lotus in Kali's hand, I wanted to blame those who were giggling for making this boy nervous. I was annoyed and angry that they were teasing someone who didn't deserve it."

"This boy was not innocent to what he received. Our unspoken thoughts can affect others, just as our physical and verbal actions can affect others," Auntie explained. "The boy was critical of himself. Those giggling were also critical of something within them. Outwardly, there appeared to be a victim and an oppressor. Inwardly, everyone acted from a place of emotional pain. When the boy felt the joy of his divine heart where critical thoughts do not exist, he didn't even notice any giggling that continued.

"The mind acts as a judge to what is right and wrong. It wants to battle what it thinks is wrong. Kali wanted to show you battle is not necessary. She distracted you from your annoyance, and you allowed yourself to receive her joyful love. You changed your inner experience to joy, and everything outside changed to joy. Others, including the boy, chose to receive your joy. There was no force, no effort, and no desire to gain power over others and control their behavior."

I recalled how the boy who played Lord Shiva talked about his ability to control the most potent of all emotions, which is fear. He even wore a serpent around his neck as a symbol of what he conquered through his control. I asked why Shiva believed it was important to control fear.

"Deep within the roots of Lord Shiva's lotus, the potential for fear exists," Nani said. "This potential shows itself in his need to control fear. But nothing with energy will remain under control forever. There will always be more battle."

I wanted to ask more questions about the violent stories of Kali I had read, but as I was about to speak, Nani said she wanted to get back to her painting now. "I need to paint a picture of Kali before I am ready to share more with you."

There was no sense arguing with them about anything. It was not worth any effort on my part to try to convince them to go against their wishes. When they got up from the table, they were done. "Perhaps it was best they stopped," I thought, feeling tightness in my body, while standing up. "It would probably be a good idea to loosen up a bit by shooting arrows at Auntie's archery range." So, I did just that.

Auntie's archery range was part of her magical castle and the best range in the village in my opinion. Just like inside her house, I saw light beings hang out there. Auntie loved archery, and I thought she was the most skilled person in our village. She told me shooting arrows helped to keep her from getting distracted by things that were not important. "I always feel into the space where I want the arrow to go. In my mind's eye, I see a distance between myself and the target. Focusing on the target, I expand my awareness into the space of my heart's sight to bring the target to me. Through the eye of my divine heart, space and time do not exist. So, there is no distance between me and the target. When I allow this expansion with complete focus, my fingers open to release the arrow from the bow when I intuitively feel it is time. The arrow follows the flow of my heart's sight." Simple words to say, but not so easy to master.

Two

Almost two weeks passed, and Nani and Auntie remained occupied with their paintings. To my great dismay, they were not the least bit interested in talking about Kali. Feeling too unfocused and restless to paint, I spent much time at Auntie's archery range. Everything got lost to me except my own center as I aimed at the target. What Auntie shared about bringing the target to her became more natural. My bow seemed to respond to my touch as I became one with it. I was far from having the expertise of Auntie, but with practice, I was determined to achieve her mastery.

When I went to visit this afternoon, I saw Nani's unfinished painting of Kali on her easel placed close to the table. Her painting was very different from Kali's statue in the temple. Kali's sword was at her feet. A dove replaced her sword in her upper left hand. Light flowed from the dove, covering the head in Kali's hand under it. Its eyes were black with compassion, and a quiet calm rested on its face. A lotus, with both light and dark throughout it, was in one of Kali's right hands. She stood on a coiled serpent instead of her husband, Lord Shiva. Its tranquil smile and compassionate, black eyes like those in the head, made it far less fearful than the serpents in Kali's statue.

"I love your painting, Nani. I don't think my friends would be afraid of Kali if they saw it." As I looked at Kali, her joyful presence invited me to play with her. Receiving her joy, Nani's painting began to vibrate with life. The serpent's gentle, compassionate black eyes told me to never fear what it offered. Then it invited me to enter its discerning eyes. Peering deeply into them, while taking a deep breath of surrender into the compassion the serpent's vision held, my vision was no longer mine alone.

Now seeing through the serpent's eyes, a light beam at the center of the lotus caught my attention. It changed the dark into the light, and the light into the dark. It was as if the light and dark were not separate at all. At times, the light and dark merged together to become a single, translucent beam of light at the center of the lotus. This light beam appeared to extend itself into the universe, and beyond, into Infinity.

The eyes of the dove radiated this translucent light beam, which duplicated itself endless times to create a majestic waterfall of light that gracefully flowed from its eyes over the head beneath it. As its water flowed, it became tiny droplets of crystals radiating the colors of a rainbow with vibrant transparency. I wanted to merge with its magnificence. As if to acknowledge my deep passion, this light flowed over my body, covering it in a blanket of bliss. I was aware only of the intensity of this luminous light radiating its endless depth of loving joy.

"Aditi," I heard Nani say slowly and gently, "Aditi, speak to me."

Hearing Nani's gentle voice, I eased my attention back into my body. Slowly, I felt my body in the chair I sat on. When my eyes opened to acknowledge Nani's request, I saw the playful twinkle in her eyes dancing.

Seeing I needed more time to regain my attention to her, Nani continued to speak gently and softly. "We saw you were enjoying Kali's joyful play. There was light flowing from the eyes of the dove over your head as a gentle waterfall of the purest crystals. Its brilliant colors held immense beauty."

"Nani, the waterfall of light was so magnificent. I lost myself in its splendor. It was as if I was that light. I was no longer in my body or here with you and Auntie."

"You experienced the intense space of pure light where space and time, as you know them to exist, are not present," Nani told me. "All that ever was, and ever can be, is within this space of translucent light. It is the deepest essence of your beingness. We brought you out of this light because its great beauty leads some to leave this planet if their minds and bodies are unprepared to receive it. You are not yet prepared for such Mastery, but you are taking courageous steps to do so."

I shared all I experienced, including the beam of pure light at the center of the lotus, which I did not notice at the school play.

"This light beam is wisdom," Auntie said through the compassion I so loved in her eyes. "The serpent carries the deepest knowledge of who we really are. It transcends the opposing forces of creation's light and dark to embrace the wisdom of the divine heart. It is aware of itself as a form within creation's duality, but knows it is much more than its physical form alone. It does not empower its opposites as its Truth. It does not get entangled in battles between the light and dark."

"When I looked into the eyes of the serpent, I felt your compassion, Auntie."

"When we allow a deep compassion for ourselves, its unconditional love dissolves the deep roots of our darkness," Auntie responded. "Light fills the space that once held pain and suffering."

"It seemed the light and the dark weren't really separate. They played together as they became the other."

"The mind was birthed in creation's duality. So, it perceives separation between opposites as a truth. But like the serpent, the mind can transcend its entanglements with duality. The serpent helps us to realize wisdom by devouring poisons in our mind and body that are our conditioned thoughts that hold charged emotions. As it ingests these poisons, beliefs that create pain and suffering are shed, just as the serpent sheds its outer layers of skin many, many times."

My attention was again drawn to Nani's painting. Its pulsating vibrations that gave it life were still there. Kali's sword at her feet made me uncomfortable. "How can Kali be compassionate if she can watch suffering?"

"Like Lord Shiva, Kali once believed it was her duty to protect others from the dark with her light. One day, as she attempted to prepare for a huge battle she and Shiva were to lead, she felt deep exhaustion and could not put her armor on. Shiva heard of Kali's difficulty and went to her bed chamber to give her encouragement."

I felt the breathing, pulsating vibrations of Nani's painting again present within the space of my heart, sharing their vision with me. The voices of Shiva and Kali slowly replaced Auntie's voice. Shiva's presence in his full armor was stunning. The emotional strength of his warrior energy felt far stronger than the physical suit of armor he wore. Kali's presence was very different. Almost as tall as Shiva, the build of her body, and how her eyes met Shiva's eyes, suggested great strength in her mind and body, just as Nani's eyes did. But now her body did not seem to have strength, and I recognized her deep desire to find it.

Shiva stood in front of the chair Kali was sitting on. "Kali, are you ill?" His voice held a gentle strength as he addressed his wife.

"I do not know why I feel such exhaustion," Kali responded through a weakened voice, "but I am unable to lift my heavy armor and cannot wear it."

Shiva never saw Kali look so vulnerable. Wanting her to be the strong warrior he knew her to be, his voice lost its gentleness as he commanded her to gather strength. "Kali, you must remember your honor as a warrior. Our forces are ready to move after weeks of preparation. A true warrior overcomes any weakness. You must be that warrior, now! Concentrate on the strength my light holds and receive it into your mind and body."

I felt Kali's attempt to concentrate on Shiva's light that flowed to her, but her body was too weak to receive the strength he offered. "Forgive me my husband, but I need a day or two to rest. Go to the army and start the journey. I will join you by week's end." Kali turned her eyes away from Shiva.

Shiva reluctantly accepted the situation. "We will be together by the end of the week," he said in his strong, commanding voice.

Kali collapsed onto her bed the moment Shiva left. She entered a deep sleep as she yielded to her exhaustion. Now fully merged with her energy, I entered Kali's dream reality with her. In her dream, Shiva stood beside Kali, dressed in his full armor. As her dream body, Kali stood tall. She breathed deeply, while opening her beingness to receive the full strength of Shiva's light. Shiva appeared pleased he could now assist his wife.

But as Kali received Shiva's warrior strength, she noticed the bold, elaborate painting of the serpent on his helmet. From the serpent's eyes flowed a light that held not a strength to conquer, but a strength to surrender to its compassion. It was the compassion I often felt flowing from Auntie's eyes. Feeling the serpent's invitation to go within, Kali blocked Shiva's light from entering her. Instead, she allowed the serpent's light to enter her and blend with her energy.

Shiva's eyes turned from pleasure to pain as he witnessed Kali blocking his light. "Kali, why do you reject my help?

You need my light to regain your strength as the warrior you are. I demand you receive it and join me in battle!"

Kali steadied herself as she breathed the compassionate energy of the serpent ever deeper within. Space opened within the cavities of her body as if to welcome the presence of this expanded breath with a space to breathe within. The serpent's deep compassion now spoke through her, just like the compassion Auntie speaks through. "No Shiva. I cannot join you in battle now. I must myself retreat. Please, leave me."

The last thing I saw was Shiva's stunned face as the vision left me. I was quite disoriented as if shaken from a deep sleep. The light beings often invited me to share their imagination, and I always needed time to adjust afterward. What Kali shared entered a space deeper inside me, and I needed more time to adjust. Nani and Auntie were sitting quietly. Their eyes lacked their sharp focus. I knew they also witnessed what I saw. Nani got up to get us a glass of water, which we drank slowly.

Kali's pain, and her effort to find strength to concentrate on the serpent's compassionate eyes, remained with me. I continued to breathe the serpent's compassion through me. Its beauty soothed and massaged the pain. "I felt so much pain in Kali," I found myself sharing. "Kali knew Shiva would not understand her choice, and her words did upset Shiva. But I also felt the compassionate strength in the serpent's eyes that Kali allowed. I don't think Kali could have turned away from Shiva without that compassion."

"Kali was confused by her choice. The compassion in the serpent's eyes awakened a knowing of a deeper Truth within. She trusted what it asked of her," Auntie said. "Kali withdrew to go deep inside herself, to touch and accept the depths of her own dark nature, through this compassion. In time, she embraced the totality of her darkness with deep compassion for All-that-is. All opposing forces of creation were released from Kali's beingness when she surrendered her battles to embrace wisdom. As time passed, her trust in this wisdom deepened, allowing its breath of light to expand ever deeper within her beingness. Kali's wisdom now shines its radiance equally on the light and the dark. She knows others must find their own courage to realize this inner wisdom."

"Why didn't Shiva feel the serpent's compassion and question his battles?" I asked.

"We feel only what our hearts are capable of feeling. We believe only what our minds are willing to believe," Nani responded to give Auntie a break. "Kali questioned her truths to allow her heart to feel a deeper Truth. Lord Shiva continues to take great pride in being a warrior who protects himself and others against the force of the dark with his light. He is not ready to surrender to a compassion that unveils what is hidden within the dark roots of his inner lotus. Someday, he will recognize the illusion of his pride and surrender all that keeps him bound in creation's polarities. Through this great act of courage that lovingly forgives and honors what has been, he will embrace his deepest Truth."

"Kali's statue in the temple can look so terrifying to others. It makes them believe fear is very real, and they must protect themselves from evil by doing battle. We are taught that freedom from fear is through control over fear. Our human ego and its fears must be slayed."

"Kali's wisdom demands recognition through the divine heart, not the human heart. The fears and doubts of the human heart must be embraced in love to feel Kali's compassionate wisdom. This wisdom does not empower fear, and its need to control through force."

I thought of how my sister Pari and Mother stayed a distance from Kali's statue, just as my friends did. They had great physical beauty, but their words did not dance with light. Last week when I shared that someone called my Auntie a witch, Mother's attention went someplace deep inside her. Her eyes looked far away, lost in a painful memory. I heard her speak to my father that night about what I was told. The tone of Father's voice was worried as he said to Mother, "Maryam, it's time that Aditi learn about Nani and Auntie. The teasing could get worse. She can understand the truth now. We both know our daughter is wise beyond her years. She won't be disturbed by teasing if she knows the truth." The following day, Mother asked Nani to speak to me about our family's past. It was time for me to know its secrets.

Three

Today was Sunday, and I was free of my responsibilities. Usually, Nani and I went to Auntie's house early to make a special breakfast. It was my most favorite meal that I looked forward to all week. Today, I believed that Nani and Auntie wanted to share their past, and I was with anticipation and worry. I was unusually quiet helping to cook and barely touched my breakfast. Nani suggested that perhaps I needed to receive only the love my food was prepared with. I nodded my head in agreement. After we cleaned up and took my remaining food outside to feed the animals, we found our way back to the table. My heart began to shrivel with fear.

Nani, not allowing my heart to close, snapped me out of my fear with her robust voice. "Aditi, if you want to know the past, then you must leave your thoughts behind and listen to our words sing within your heart. If we see you restless or distracted, you are no longer hearing accurately what needs to be shared, and we will end the sharing for the day."

Nani and Auntie looked deep into my eyes, touching my heart with the light their eyes held. I allowed this light to fill me as I breathed it deeply within. All worry and concern left. Nani and Auntie were Masters of transcending space and time. When I surrendered to their presence, they shared their Mastery with me. If I allowed my emotions, I would no longer be present in their clearness. The light in my eyes would fade, and Nani's voice with it. I checked my posture and concentration, while surrendering even deeper into the space their eyes held.

"Like you," Nani began, "I saw the nature spirits and light beings. Such endless joy I knew playing with them. When I was very small, people barely noticed how occupied I was with my playmates. But when I entered school, and still talked to them, the teachers told my parents I should have outgrown my imaginary friends. They suggested something was wrong with me."

Slowly, as she continued to speak, I was taken to the time and place of the event being shared. I remained aware of my physical form sitting in the chair, but I was also aware beyond my body. I did not need my physical ears because I heard through my heart's knowing. I saw a girl about my age, who I recognized as the younger body of my Nani Mishka. She was listening to her mother and father speak to her.

"Mishka," Nani's father said in a tone that was firm, but filled with tenderness, "you must accept that the beings you see are only in your imagination. They are not real. You will bring embarrassment to yourself and the family if you continue to insist that they are real."

Nani's mother nodded in agreement. "Your father and I don't want to cause you pain. We only want what is best for you. You must see how your friends respond to you in puzzlement when you speak to these nature spirits and nonphysical beings. They have moved on to learn how to cooperate with human beings of the real world. When you believe these beings are speaking to you, you must tell them you now know they are not real, and to leave your presence."

I witnessed how the words of my Nani's parents broke her heart. But I also felt their shared love, and Nani's deep desire to please them. Searching for strength, Nani told them this behavior would never happen again. She would do as asked and tell the light beings to leave her presence.

I watched with dreaded anticipation as Nani went to her bedroom. Alone in her room, she breathed deeply, while opening her heart. She called in the nature spirits and light beings she so loved. "I am directed to tell you that you must all leave. You are of my imagination, and I must not continue to pretend that you are real."

Breaking into deep sobs, she ordered them to leave her, and they did as she directed. In their parting, I saw the light beings radiate an understanding to Nani that should she again wish their presence shared with her, they would joyfully return. These beings never used words to communicate because they were without a body and its mouth. I knew their light seamlessly flowed from their heart to my heart, only if I allowed it to be received. I saw the beings I so loved leave her as Nani continued to bid them farewell through her sobs.

Slowly, my awareness left that time and space and returned to the room where I sat with Auntie and Nani. When I looked at them, the intense gaze of their eyes softened. It was time to stop. I saw their faces as they presently are. Tears filled my eyes, but I was puzzled about what I saw and felt. While I shared the imagination of light beings and mythic figures, I had never witnessed past life events of people I knew. They saw my puzzlement.

Auntie, who also witnessed this part of Nani's past, gave voice to my concerns. "You are confused about what you just witnessed and questioning if it was real. The mind knows a past, present, and future that exist in ordered time. But the divine heart knows the fullness of the present moment that is without ordered time. All that has been, and all potentials of what can be, are simultaneously present. When your eyes looked within ours, you allowed an expansion of your beingness into the space of the divine heart. We could then bring your attention to this part of Nani's past."

"Pari must know of this. Yet, she has not shared it with me. Was she asked to keep this silent?" I asked, attempting to make what I just witnessed more real to me.

Auntie explained that Pari and I each had our own destinies. Like Mother, Pari had great beauty in her physical features, but her heart was not of the divine heart. While Pari was a loving person, it was a love of the human heart and its changing emotions. "Your mother and I shared a few details of the past as Pari needed to hear them. The radiance you carry demands a clarity that touches your divine heart. We told Pari we would speak to you when you are ready to hear the past. Out of respect and love for all of us, she kept quiet."

I now understood why my entire beingness was absorbed in the moment when I was with Nani and Auntie. But when I was not with them, I sometimes became emotional as well. I relive something in the past and critically judge myself and others. "There are times when I'm not in this house that I get upset. The joy I so easily feel here becomes difficult to find."

"It is natural for the mind to feel confused about what is real, and what is unreal, as it matures," Auntie offered. "Over the next few years, if you choose to face the depths of your fear and other emotions, there will be times of great upset. To acknowledge all parts of you, while allowing the heart's compassion to cleanse your dark emotions, is a courageous act of trust."

Feeling Nani's sadness when she released the light beings from her presence, I wondered if she acted without truthfulness in that moment. I distracted her from her reverie to answer my question. "Nani, did you really believe these light beings were unreal? Didn't you have the opportunity to speak your truth to your parents and not order them to leave?"

"At first, their words were difficult to accept, but I deeply loved them and didn't want embarrassment to come to them because of me. For the first time, I experienced doubt of what is real, and what is unreal. With the nature spirits and light beings gone, I came to accept their words as truth and stopped seeing them. I accepted the beliefs and values of my community. I thought I was living life as it should be lived. I thought I understood who I really was, and what truth really was. But I always felt an emptiness within me after that day."

Nani's gaze lost its focus as she returned to the memory of that time. It was rare to witness emotions in her, but that memory pulled her into the sadness of the moment. I was about to get up and shoot some arrows when Auntie began to speak again. This time, it was me who suggested we stop until tomorrow. I felt Nani's sorrow so deeply that I wanted to sob for her. I needed some space. Auntie followed me to the archery range. As I settled into my practice, she offered tips for improvement.

Everyone except Himmat and Nani seemed out of sorts this morning. Pari did not feel well. She complained of a low fever and headache, and Mother told her to stay in bed for the day. Father complained of a restless sleep. Contrary to his unwavering demeanor, he paced impatiently waiting for his chai. Mother wore a worried frown on her face and could not find the flour she needed. She asked Father to please stop pacing.

I felt that at any moment I would burst from all the tension as I prepared the chai as quickly as possible. Nani, in her usual calm and collected manner, found the flour right where it always was. After handing it to Mother, she put her hands on my shoulders for a minute or so. As mother handed a cup of chai to Father, she finally asked what was bothering him.

"Maryam, I cannot understand why business was so poor this month," Father said with an unusual tension in his voice. "For six months, we made more profit than we ever did. How could business have been so poor last month? Perhaps we were not generous enough to the temple priest with our monthly contribution. If we become greedy, the natural flow of give and take of money will be disrupted. Sharing our profits with others less fortunate will keep greed out of our lives. I want to make a generous offering to the temple this month."

Mother poured herself a cup of chai as she considered Father's suggestion. "Perhaps you're right," she replied after being silent for a few moments. "We were blessed with good fortune. We do not want bad karma to enter our lives because we neglected to share our blessings with others. Offer what you believe is an appropriate amount."

Father nodded in agreement as he went into his office to take care of the contribution before his daily trip to the temple for worship. Mother and I gathered the clothes to bring to the river for washing. Nani appeared to be rushing to clean the kitchen. Before Father left, he asked Nani if she would help Auntie with a special clothing order that he wanted finished today.

I immersed myself into the dance of the sun's light onto the water to feel its joy dance within me as I washed clothes this morning. The sunrise of the morning never lost its magical spell on me. The light beings usually remained with me when I was in school, but I was too distracted to be with them today. Instead, I counted the minutes left as soon as I got to school. After school, I completed my afternoon chores in much the same manner, ignoring the beings that wanted to play. I arrived at Auntie's house earlier than usual.

Nani was there since morning, helping Auntie complete the order Father wanted done. They finished their work just as I arrived. Nani started to clean up, and Auntie did her usual job of making chai. I helped Nani clean up this time, trying to hurry her along. I also needed to bring the clothing order to the house for a worker to pick up. Soon all jobs were completed, and we were ready to join each other at the table. The sadness in Nani's eyes was gone, and she began to share more about sending the light beings away.

"When I was a young child, my soul's spirit breathed Its expansive breath through the quiet spaciousness of my mind and body, expressing Its joyful magic through me. But as I matured, this open space slowly contracted into a space crowded with the beliefs and strong emotions of others. Their energies filled the empty space within me, and they became my truth. My breath became shallow, breathing through the crowded space of these heavy beliefs. My spirit's breath that needed quiet, open space to breathe through, could no longer be present. Like Kali, a time came when I retreated inward to embrace my darkness with compassion to resolve its pain. Only then, could my mind and body create through my spirit's joy."

As Nani talked, I thought about the open space by the river that was changing. "Our village crowds the open space around the river with more buildings and loud activity each year. People don't seem to care about the nature that is being destroyed. I feel the heaviness of the noise and escape into my play with the joy of the nature spirits and light beings. I see sadness in the eyes of most adults, including Mother and

Father. I saw sadness in the eyes of the boy who was singing out of tune. Even Pari's eyes sometimes carry a sadness that was not there before. "

"Your mind is uncluttered with the noisy chatter of emotional thoughts, so you experience the magic of a pure heart and mind. Your sensitivity to the chatter of people's thoughts makes you feel their heaviness. People are unaware of the weight their thoughts and emotions carry, just as I was once ignorant to. They fill their empty sadness with things of the world, but the fear that underlies much of their behavior robs them of true joy and creativity. That is why I look so serious in old photos of myself that caught your attention when you were younger."

"Nani, you were in the kitchen this morning when my parents were speaking about their temple contribution. Did you feel Father's tension and see the fear in his eyes? I thought I would burst from it."

Nani nodded to indicate a yes. "They want to show compassion to others and are charitable. But their need to bring only good karma to themselves motivates much of their giving. Your father fears what may happen to disturb the happiness of his family, and the profit of his business. He's unaware of his tension as he tries to control forces that he believes may impact your lives."

"Are you telling me that karma isn't real? Aren't Father's charitable actions important for the poor?"

"Karma is real only when we deny the presence of the heart's wisdom," Nani said, while looking at me carefully to be sure I was following her. "Without wisdom, we see a world with good and bad, and right and wrong, and all the endless opposites of positive and negative forces. Efforts are made to bring only good into our lives by doing good toward others. If someone does harm to us, we believe we must take revenge. The mind acts and reacts. Its roots are fear, and fear creates the need for safety. Wisdom is beyond the harm of any person or thing. It's the grace of the magician that sees right through fear."

I wondered what happened in the past that enabled Nani to allow grace back into her life. But it was not my choice when she would share more about her life. Nani's words about compassion reminded me about the serpent on Shiva's helmet that so captivated me. I wanted to try to capture its fearless compassion in a painting and quickly finished my chai to start it.

Four

A week passed since Nani and Auntie shared their past, and I was occupied with their words. I visited Auntie's magical castle to paint as much as possible. I wanted to work on Lord Shiva's serpent. Even more important, was the playful light there that helped me get distance from my worries. My mind wanted to evaluate their words. It wanted factual answers, but the answers would not come through the facts my mind related to. Auntie and Nani would speak from their hearts, to my heart, when it was ready to receive their words.

There were a few details I knew about my family's past, but they were a sketch yet to be filled in. Nani said her mother had the beauty of my mother. She was a devoted wife and mother and involved herself in many community activities. She suffered from asthma, and a bad case of the flu turned into pneumonia. She died when Nani was a young adult and already married. Her father worked at a village print shop as a typesetter. He was loyal to the traditions of the community, but Nani said she felt a tenderness in him that she did not feel in other men. When Nani's mother died, her father's light-hearted spirit became heavy with sadness. Nani believed his sadness ate away at his human heart, until he died of a heart attack three years later.

Dadi, Nani's husband, was a clerk with the government in a larger village a distance from where we lived. He took a bus to and from work every day. The buses were without heat and air conditioning. He worked long hours six days a week, and the bus ride added to the challenges of his workday. Dadi was quite overweight because he loved sweets and fried foods. Nani encouraged him to change his poor eating habits, but he did not listen. Nani knew he disliked his work and ate the foods he did to make his days more enjoyable. Even the bus ride back and forth from work challenged him. The stifling summer heat settled in, often giving him headaches. The cold of the winter chilled him to the bones.

Nani said she used to worry about things like Dadi's health, but his humor made her laugh about her worries. He never complained, even though Nani believed he had much to complain about. He was a family man and enjoyed every free moment he had with them. I saw Dadi's playfulness in a photo of him and Nani when I was younger. Nani's face and eyes were heavy with seriousness. When I asked Nani why she looked so serious, she told me she had not "awakened" yet.

"But Nani, your eyes are wide open," I replied with confusion.

"My eyes were physically open, but I had yet to awaken into my divine heart. I saw only what my mind wanted me to see. I was asleep to a greater Truth within. You will understand my words when your heart is ready to understand them."

Dadi died of a sudden stroke on an unusually hot, humid summer night shortly after he returned home from work. My mother was just entering her teen years, and Auntie was a young girl. Nani had her moments of grief, but she accepted Dadi's death. She did her best to show strength to my future mother and Auntie. She believed if she lived without fear for the future, her daughters would also be less likely to feel fear.

Nani later shared she knew death was only the dropping of the body because our soul continues to live on, even when not in a body. "Shortly after Dadi's death, I began to feel his presence at times, nudging me out of my grief and fears," Nani shared when I asked if she missed Dadi. "But a time came when we understood we must set each other free of our emotional attachments, and dependencies on each other, as husband and wife. There was a greater love for each to discover within, even if Dadi was without a body to do so."

When I looked quite puzzled, Nani assured me that as I matured into a woman, I would better understand. "Love's deepest echo cannot be known through the words of others. One must uncover layers of noisy confusion to feel its joy dance within the depthless, soundless chamber of our divine heart."

When I asked Father about his past, he shared that those before me worked hard when on this Earth. He wanted to ensure their peaceful rest by not speaking of things that could upset their departed souls. I knew that Father's grandfather, my Paradada, was ambitious. He loved cloth and clothing and was regarded as the best-dressed male in our village. He worked as often as he could to save money to start his own clothing store. In time, his dream to have his own cloth shop came to be. His shop slowly grew, as his reputation for being an outstanding tailor grew. In pictures I saw of him, every detail of his slim appearance appeared perfected. I saw pride in his eyes, and in how he held his body when the picture was taken.

Dada, the father of my father, inherited a love for clothing. He also inherited the ambition of his father. He continued to build the shop business after his father passed. Dada loved his father and wanted the shop to grow in his name. All the love, time, and effort given to help the shop grow into something even grander, gave birth to exactly what Dada dreamed of. His only distraction was the woman he married and deeply loved.

Nana and Dada were said to be inseparable. She sewed for Dada's shop and became quite skilled through his encouraging guidance. Their wedding picture showed a joyful couple, impeccably dressed. Nana's eyes were gentle and kind, and Dada's eyes were very much like Father's eyes. Dada's eyes were kind, but they also revealed seriousness. I understood where Father's discipline and deep sense of duty to family came from.

Hredhann, Father's name, was the only child of Nana and Dada. His birth was difficult on Nana's body who was a diabetic, and she could not have more children. My future father also learned to sew, but he lacked his parents' gift of design. Father was more inclined mathematically, and he took over most of the shop's financial concerns when he was only 14. Dada was delighted his artistic talents did not have to be sacrificed to the daily financial matters of the shop.

My grandparents had been loyal friends since their teenage years. When Dadi died, Dada hired Nani to sew for the shop. He knew Dadi's parents lived with his sister's family who had been ill for many years. Nani would be alone and need help paying bills. Working from home, she did not have to leave her daughters alone. Nani had two brothers who visited frequently, but their ability to help financially was limited. Knowing the reputation of Dada's shop, they asked Nani if she would teach them how to sew. Mother also showed an interest in sewing and often assisted Nani. With unused pieces of cloth, Mother made accessories for others. She bought cloth to make her own clothes with the money made. She was slowly gaining a reputation as a talented seamstress and designer.

Mother and Father enjoyed each other's company as children when their families got together for various events. Their friendship grew even deeper after Dadi died, and Nani worked for Dada. They looked for opportunities to take materials to and from the shop to see each other. One day, when Mother was in an unusually playful mood as we washed clothes, she shared how much she loved Father since she first set eyes on him as a young girl. "I can't even begin to count the number of times I told your Nani that Hredhann was the right man for me to marry," she shared with a warm smile. "I was ecstatic when I was told my wish to marry your father would come true. He has proven even more kind and generous than I believed he was."

Once the engagement between my parents was formally agreed upon and announced, Dada frequently invited Mother to his shop to share the secrets of design his father had shared with him. When Mother married Father, she moved into Father's family house. Dada bought the latest model sewing machine for her. Mother cherished that machine, just as she increasingly cherished her relationship with her new father-in-law. Mother created designs for women's clothing that delighted Dada and the customers. Sadly, about a year after Father and Mother married, Dada lost his life in a tragic train accident when returning home with new cloth. Father was only 20 years old, but he assumed full responsibility for the shop's business.

Nana's grief for her loss of Dada was immense, and it began to stress the household. Her diabetes worsened because she was no longer willing to take proper care of herself. She appeared to have willed herself to die, and her health quickly deteriorated. Mother's attempts to convince Nana of the importance of self-care were fruitless. In addition to Mother's grief from the loss of a person she cherished and the added demands of taking care of Nana, she was also suffering from frequent nausea. The doctor informed her that within seven months, she and my father would be parents. Father's sharp focus was lost to his grief and his worries for his mother and wife. Sewing orders from the shop were piling up, and the customers were getting restless. They needed help and decided to ask Nani and Auntie to move in with them.

Nani willingly agreed to move in. Auntie was excited about living with her sister again. Nani's house was sold, and Father's house remodeled to ensure everyone's comfort. A private space of her own was a condition Nani gave to the move. Nani's two brothers were hired as tailors. With Nani and Auntie now living there, and extra help for the shop, Father and Mother could focus on getting back orders filled. Mother could also give herself the necessary time for her own self-care. But Nani could do little to help Father's mother out of her depression and waning health. Nana's body knew she wished to die, and its cells responded accordingly, slowly shutting its organs down. Within a year of Dada's death, she passed.

As the difficulties of the past year were gracefully met and eased, respectful relationships within the household deepened. Father, grateful for Nani's strong but flexible disposition, now regarded her as a treasured part of the family. She filled a space of loss that helped all to heal. The household found a new rhythm that knew few conflicts. But the trust and respect that had grown between Father and Nani would be tested in the disruption that soon entered their lives. It was this disruption that explained why a separate house was built for Auntie where she now lived. I knew I would soon learn what this disruption was.

That was how life was lived in our village. When married, the bride moved into the groom's family home. Families lived together and grew old together. The women accepted the duties of taking care of elderly parents, husbands, and children, as well as all household chores that came with the daily life of many people living under one roof. The men accepted responsibility for the financial means to support the family.

The values of the temple scriptures were ingrained in us from one generation to the next. However, people loved to gossip. It seemed easier to speak the words of the scripture than to live them, even with the fear of creating bad karma by gossiping. "Fear needs energy to create and sustain its life force," I recalled Nani saying. "It's an escalating thundercloud, accumulating strength by sucking life energy from what surrounds it."

I pulled myself out of my reverie as I completed the last of my responsibilities for the day. I sensed Nani and Auntie were going to share more with me today. Somewhat hesitantly, I made my way to Auntie's house to find them already sitting at her small table. They made my favorite biscuits, so I knew what was to follow. Auntie shared a funny story about something that happened that day as we drank our chai. When the table was cleared, it was not necessary for them to remind me of my responsibility with my concentration and focus. Nodding I was ready, my eyes met their eyes. I was again taken to a space in the past where Mother, Auntie, and Nani were present.

Nani was a much younger woman, and Auntie was about a year younger than I was now. They were together in the kitchen. I saw my future mother run inside to get something from her bedroom. A couple of her friends remained outside. When she heard Nani speaking to Auntie, she hid to listen, unaware Nani knew she was listening nearby. Nani looked tense and unsure of herself, just as in her photo with Dadi. The magic her eyes now held was not there, appearing more like Mother's eyes than the playful eyes I now knew. There were rice and sorting bowls on the kitchen counter. Nani appeared to be taking a break from sifting through the rice to clean it.

As their voices came alive in the room, I heard Auntie telling Nani about the light beings she saw. Auntie's eyes were alive with magic, but they lacked the compassion I now knew. Nani appeared to be half listening, anxious to return to her work. Auntie sensed her lack of interest and did not persist. When she stopped speaking, Nani began speaking, "Kiara, when I was about your age, I also saw light beings and nature spirits. It is comfortable to stay with our childhood fantasies, but you are getting older now. It is best to accept that they are not real. If you continue to speak to them, others will begin to question if there is something wrong with you. Maryam has realized they are not real. She is listening, and I'm sure she would agree with me that they are not real."

A bit surprised Nani knew she was present and listening, my mother emerged from what she thought was her hiding spot. Mother was also somewhat dark-skinned, which enhanced the beauty of her facial features. Even though she was in play clothes, they draped her body in a way that made her look like a royal queen, just as the clothes on Pari's body looked at times. I felt Mother's love for her little sister, and her desire not to hurt her with words. She seemed to rehearse her words before speaking to Auntie. "It's true, Kiara. The light beings you love so much are imaginary friends. I have many friends in physical bodies that you and I can see, touch, and play with. You like my friends, and you will make your own friends with physical bodies as well. I can help you."

The gentle magic I initially saw dancing in Auntie's eyes yielded to an intense desperation as she pleaded with my future mother and Nani. "Please, listen to me! My light friends are more real than anyone I know with bodies that I can touch and see. What they share is so alive with joy. I see waves of light come from them that touch me with love. Do not ask me to leave their presence, please."

Mother and Nani lowered their gaze from Kiara as all hearts throbbed with pain. Nani pierced the heavy silence with a gentle, but firm voice. "Kiara, one day you will understand that our actions were for your benefit. I am your mother, and I must guide you to grow into a healthy woman physically, emotionally, and spiritually. Maryam and I have no other choice than to continually remind you that your friends are not real. Do not give them any of your attention. If you do not give them attention, then you will come to understand they exist only in the imagination of your childhood. You have grown out of childhood now. A part of that growth is letting go of your imaginary friends."

When Nani and my mother stopped speaking, I saw great sadness and resignation in Auntie's eyes. She accepted what was necessary to be done. Nani showed great resolve in her request, and Kiara knew she must honor it.

Slowly, I became aware of my surroundings with Nani and Auntie as I knew them today. I was grateful I was spared watching Auntie Kiara send the light beings away. It was enough to witness Nani's farewell to them. No one wanted to speak. Auntie got up to go outside to the archery range, and I followed. With trepidation, I thought of listening to more in another week. While I did not know if I could bear witnessing any more heartache, I did want to know the events that changed Nani and Auntie.

Five

Almost every day this past week, Nani and Auntie arranged a special activity to do together. We made different kinds of treats, played games at the archery range, and even danced one day. Gradually, the anxiousness I felt last week was replaced with an impatient desire to better understand the two women I deeply loved. I barely touched the special treat that signified the invitation to be present with them to share the past. When the chai was finished, and the light in their eyes met mine, I found myself at a celebration in the village temple. The temple looked much as it does today, with only minor changes in its appearance.

I recognized many faces that were much younger than what I now knew. The immense joy present as people celebrated the Festival of Lights, tested the strength of the temple walls to contain it within its structure without bursting. It was as if all the temple gods had conspired to open the hearts of people that night to know a joy few ever experienced. A small group of musicians played beautiful music, while almost everyone danced to its playful rhythm. A few women were in the kitchen preparing the feast that was to follow. Nani was one of those women.

My attention moved to my future mother, who looked like a beautiful goddess. She was dancing with a man who I recognized as her husband, and my future father. I could see that Mother would soon give birth to Pari. Auntie Kiara looked about 15 years old. She was also dancing with a young man. I sensed she was not married to him, but I couldn't help noticing the love dancing between them. I wondered if plans had been made for them to marry. As people danced, the energy in the temple spiraled into ever more expanded, white light. I had never witnessed such light in the temple before. Its radiance touched the minds and bodies of all as their energy increasingly lost its harsh colors.

When this light touched Auntie, her entire beingness cried out to receive it. Her cry was answered by the goddess Kali, whose stone statue assumed an intense, glowing light. Directing her light toward Auntie, Kali's light entered through the crown of her head. This light spiraled deeper within Auntie's body as she surrendered her breath to Kali's breath of light. Melding with the glow of Kali's pulsating light, the solid parts of Auntie's body became lucid. The rhythm of Kali's breath expressed itself through the rhythm of Auntie's dance.

A rope of light appearing as the form of a serpent emerged from Kali's navel area, extending its spiraling movement to the same area of Auntie's body. Feeling its loving touch, Auntie acknowledged it with a gentle bow to Kali's glowing statue. Moving out of her bow, this light entered through Auntie's navel area. Her eyes radiated the bliss her body was immersed within. Auntie's dance became ever more erotic. Her flowing, graceful movements blessed all through them. I was in awe, captivated by its beauty. Its hypnotic beauty made people stop their own dancing to watch her.

My future mother ran to the kitchen. "Mother, come quickly," she pleaded. "You must watch Kiara dance." All the women followed her to the dance area. Once there, they saw everyone in a trance-like state watching Auntie. Even the musicians stopped playing to watch as Kiara danced to a magical rhythm that beat deep within the hearts of all. Nani's eyes were filled with awe. The twinkle I now know in her eyes grew, while this light expanded throughout Nani's body. Tears flowed from her eyes.

The same priest who took care of the temple today, but in a much younger body, was not present where the dancing was. The priest, and another man assisting him, were in his office taking care of last-minute gifts for worshippers who helped prepare the celebration. Aroused by a curiosity of the silence, they made their way to the dance area. They were not part of the joy that opened the hearts of all watching to enable them to appreciate the beauty of Auntie's dance. Instead, they came with their judgments that saw Auntie's dance as unacceptable, both in and out of the temple. The harshness of the energy of the man assisting the priest greatly contrasted to the energy of the others.

The priest stood rigidly still, and his body became a statue. His vacant eyes on a very pale face, showed his stunned state. The man who assisted in his office was yelling at Auntie Kiara, "Stop your inappropriate dancing at once!" But Auntie's awareness had left the space of the temple room, as she shared the expanded space of Kali's light, and she could not hear him. Initially, his harsh voice touched no one. Slowly, however, as the heavy, demanding tone of his voice grew, the joy on people's faces changed to shock. They stood rigidly still, watching what was before them. Unable to stop Auntie with his words, the man was now trying to grab her arms to restrain their movement with his strength. As he did so, he continued to yell at her to stop at once.

Auntie appeared hit by a bolt of lightning when she became aware of the grasp of the man's hands on her arms, and of his voice yelling at her to stop. All color drained from her face, and her breathing became shallow, constricted, and rapid. Her frightened eyes disappeared into their eyelids as her body went into a seizure. Father and Mother froze with fear not knowing how to respond. Nani, also in a very expanded space of light, forced her awareness back into the room to assist Auntie. She asked that people go to the dining area where the feast was ready.

Attempting to overcome his own frozen state, the priest clumsily led the others to the kitchen. His slow, unbalanced gait went unnoticed. Most people were attempting to find their own center of balance as they slowly maneuvered their way to the kitchen. The anger of the man who was yelling at Auntie remained. He questioned people about how they were seduced into the enjoyment of Auntie's dance. Now serving food in his stunned state, the priest was unaware of what this man was saying.

As the people became more present in their familiar beliefs and emotions, most readily accepted the suggestion that Auntie had seduced them. I felt their emotions of shame and guilt for having allowed Auntie to do that to them. Needing a source to blame for their behavior, some declared that only a witch could have tricked them into being mesmerized by her dancing. As the gossip became more vicious, a heavy darkness began to fill the room. This darkness grew, becoming a powerful storm cloud that devoured the room's light. The eyes of most people were now filled with fear, and their voices now filled with anger. I knew the dark strength of the storm cloud was alive in them, and they would use its power to strike out at Auntie.

Auntie left the temple with Nani, Mother, and Father when the seizure ended. Mother and Father appeared stunned, but I felt their deep love and concern for Auntie. Nani, however, did not appear stunned. Rather, her deep seriousness was lifted from her as if she acknowledged a goodness in this event unacknowledged by others. Auntie was very shaken, but she was not stunned either. Both she and Nani appeared present in love, rather than fear. Kali's light had deeply touched them, but I was unable to grasp how this light transformed them. Not wanting to witness more, I asked to return to the present time.

With tears in my eyes, I was present again in Auntie's house. I sobbed for her and my family. I felt their ecstatic state of joy, followed by the need to quickly jolt themselves from their joy to adjust to the chaos and gossip that followed only moments afterward. They allowed me the time I needed to let my sobs out. It was Auntie who began to speak when I was ready to listen.

"Be joyful, Aditi. This event was the moment of awakening for me and Nani. We waited to show you this because we wanted you to understand that enlightenment is not just about feeling and embracing the light. The dark within must also be acknowledged and embraced through grace. That evening allowed us the opportunity to meet both the light and the dark at a very profound level.

"I had choices to make about how I'd handle this situation. Would I allow my own unresolved emotions to control my thoughts and actions by blaming others, and fueling gossip as I did so? Or would I face the depths of my inner darkness, so I would not project onto others what was inside of me? I allowed my heart to open to a love that knew no fear of how others judged me during my dance. But now I had to trust my heart's wisdom to guide me, and no longer let my mind's fear and other emotions guide me." Auntie stopped speaking to have a drink of water and offered me the same.

We sat quietly for some time, sipping the water to help bring our attention back into our bodies. It helped to settle me a little. "The awakening Auntie spoke of must be the light I saw that entered her and Nani's bodies when they cried out to receive it," I thought to myself as I drank my water. "They seemed so much more alive receiving the joy this light held." I was beginning to understand what Nani meant when she said she had not yet awakened in the photo with her and

Dadi. My mind and body can be wide awake, and my eyes wide open, but if I am asleep to my soul's wisdom, I am asleep to real love and joy.

Nani then spoke of how Mother and Father, also mesmerized by Auntie's dance, experienced the joy this light offered as they watched. "Once the man started to yell, and their awareness reentered the beliefs of their minds, they doubted the beauty they had witnessed. They were confused because their minds could not provide them with an acceptable explanation. They knew Auntie was not a witch who would seduce others. In time, they created a belief that it was Auntie's playful and joyful spirit that so captivated them by her dance."

"Nani, why didn't you and Auntie doubt the light like the others? I saw the energy change in almost everyone, but only you and Auntie cried out to receive the light fully into your bodies."

"This awakening was a potential for everyone there. People felt the joy, but fear kept them from surrendering more deeply into it. The deep love Auntie and I shared with the light beings for so long when younger was more potent than fear. Fear could not touch the love we opened to receive in that moment. It was fear that brought people's awareness back into their minds so quickly, once it was vividly expressed through the man's forceful yelling at Auntie to end her dance.

"Like the others, your father wanted life to return to what it was before the incident. He feared the ridicule that Auntie could be exposed to, and her ability to cope with it. He also feared the gossip that could destroy the family's honor and means of survival. He wanted it stopped. People might stop buying cloth and having clothes made at his shop. His fear was exasperated by the very recent loss of his parents. With both parents now gone, he felt overwhelmed with the responsibilities of the shop. He believed it was his duty to honor those before him by growing the shop's success.

"Your father always followed the teachings of the scriptures rigorously, which encouraged a simple, charitable life. The money he gave to the temple prior to Auntie's dance had established a good relationship with the priest. He knew the priest would not want to lose his financial support that helped to sustain the costs of the temple and its activities.

"Now with a plausible explanation for Auntie's behavior, your father was ready to speak to the priest. Recognizing the tension that he held, your father asked me to accompany him to the temple. The priest knew me well, and your father thought my presence may help ease any tension that might interfere with resolving this issue as he wished it to be resolved. I agreed with the condition that your father spoke, not me."

Nani described the nervousness of the priest when they gathered for the meeting. She noticed how he tightly clenched his hands, and how his shoulders were pulled inward, as if to hold his tension in a safe place, while gathering strength to speak of that night. There were beads of sweat on his forehead.

Your father reminded the priest of Auntie's joyful, playful spirit that required tempering at times. He also reminded him of Auntie's love for the goddess Kali. Nani stopped for a moment as if trying to recall Father's exact words. "We all know the spirit of the goddess Kali is not tempered either, but no one calls Kali a witch and a seducer," your father explained as lightheartedly as he could. "It was a joyful night. Kiara's spirit of playfulness was seen at its extreme. We both know she is not a witch to be feared. The vicious gossip suggesting she is, must end."

Nani spoke of the tension in the voice of the priest as he asked my father to please accept his apologies and deep regret for all that took place that night. His head was lowered to avoid eye contact, and my father lowered his gaze out of respect for the space the priest required. Nani said the priest explained that he was quite stunned by the dancing. In that state, he was unaware of the gossip being spread during the feast.

The priest agreed that my father's words provided a very plausible explanation for what was witnessed. Feeling shame for the behavior of all involved, the priest expressed his anxiousness to help others understand what happened. My father was assured the gossip would stop. But the priest could not stop the gossip. People's minds, now infested with the poison of the gossip's thunderous roar, would not allow its tumultuous force living inside them to be calmed so readily.

I became distracted, as the sadness of this situation overtook me. I loved Auntie deeply, and it was difficult to accept that people thought of her as a witch. How could they have so easily fallen for such a lie? Auntie's compassionate voice pulled me out of my distress.

"Your mother and father decided it was best for me to stay out of sight until things settled down. They asked if we were comfortable that I would remain home for a while. I was glad I was not asked to leave the house, although it was seldom restful. There was always so much activity in the house with the business and your parents' friends. I felt anxious and tried to find a place to hide from them. When your father suggested building this house for me in the back, I was very excited for the space. I lacked the strength to cope with all the unspoken emotions of those visiting."

Auntie continued to share how her dance awakened a grace that she willingly denied when asked to do so as a child. The space of her own house gave her the quiet she needed to feel her divine heart and see the light beings her heart played with. But even in her own space, Auntie often felt a restlessness that concealed the quiet peace of her heart. Doubts surfaced about what she shared with Kali that night. She felt anger that the boy she loved was taken from her.

"The light beings encouraged me to find strength through the light Kali awakened within me. Only through its compassion, could my highly charged emotions find their resolution and yield to peace. Slowly, gradually, I befriended the compassionate love of my soul. Through Its love, I accepted who I am, as I am. I was maturing into the wisdom that my soul's essence is within me, as Me. There was no need to seek love and approval from others. If I did marry that boy, what remained of my darkness would limit the love

I could know and share. I would not know this deeper love that I now embody."

I looked at Auntie with such amazement. In two or three years, I would be the same age as her when the dance took place. Auntie's lack of anger for her isolation felt so brave. While I loved being at her home, I was not confined to it. I could go anywhere in the village I wanted. "You did not feel caged within these walls and its grounds?" I asked.

Peering even more deeply into my eyes, Auntie said, "I've allowed and embodied much grace within me. Through its light, I can travel anywhere I want within the universe. Why would I care if it is best not to stir the memories of others by staying out of the village? I am free, Aditi, in a way that you, too, can be free. You know that every season of the year Nani and I spend time in the forest for two weeks. Our time in the forest is enough time away for me."

"That night did much the same for me," Nani said as my attention shifted to her eyes. She continued to share that when she saw her daughter dance through Kali's grace, her heart opened to receive Kali's grace as well. She had shed tears because she experienced the beauty of this light. She knew she had erred in telling her daughter to deny her intuition and what it allowed her to see, just as her parents had erred in telling her to deny her intuition. Like Auntie, she did not want to deny this magic again, although she was often tempted to do so. The many doubts and fears of her mind teased her into believing that what she experienced was not real.

Nani went on to share her challenges that followed.

"There were times when I allowed myself to feel anger toward those who struck with harsh words. Like your parents, I believed we were victims to the oppressive words of others. I had to find the strength to keep my dignity and be cordial to customers. So, I pretended I was not bitter. I was not aware that pretending my anger did not exist, helped to dissolve it. My emotions were without the fuel needed for their survival. Like Auntie, I came to understand that the only way to know true peace, was to resolve within me, what was seeking energy outside of me. Over time, the gossip faded, and your father's shop regained its losses quickly. With Auntie out of sight of the villagers, there was seldom talk of the incident."

So much had been shared to digest, and I needed time to do so. The love I already felt for Nani and Auntie expanded beyond any measurable degree; it was without boundaries and conditions.

Six

I could hardly believe I would be 13 years old in two weeks. It was some time since Nani and Auntie went to the forest. "As you know, we go to the forest four times each year for two weeks," Nani said with a huge grin on her face as we drank our afternoon chai. "It's almost springtime, and it's a good time for your initiation into our forest adventures. As a birthday gift, we would like you to join us in the forest. We leave two weeks from today. Do you want to get permission from your parents to come along?"

You can only imagine my uncontained excitement at this possibility. When I told them that I would ask permission during dinner, Nani said she would stay at Auntie's to eat as she sometimes did. Later at dinner, I would remind my parents the invitation was offered as a gift for my upcoming birthday. They taught us to receive a gift with gratitude, so I doubted they would not allow me to go.

I seldom had long conversations with either of my parents. Pari tended to chat endlessly with Mother, but I usually had little interest in their conversations. Mother knew I talked with Nani and Auntie often and accepted the way things were. She also knew I often communicated silently with the nature spirits and light beings as she and Pari talked together. Mother trusted I would not cause embarrassment to anyone by making gestures to them, or having conversations with them, outside of Auntie's house.

During dinner, Father typically asked my brother questions about his studies. Himmat appeared to enjoy this time, pleasing both my parents with his endless intellectual insights. I took little interest in such insights. It was much more pleasant to escape into the light all about me. Tonight, I found myself impatient waiting for the usual conversation to end. Finally, all was silent. It was a silence heavy with anticipation. Clearing my throat to communicate confidence and maturity, I spoke. "Nani and Auntie invited me to go to the forest with them in a month for two weeks as a birthday gift. I must have your permission to do so."

Mother and Father looked at each other. Mother nodded a yes to Father to let him know it was fine with her, but it was an accepted tradition that Father had the final word. "You may go if you can make up the schoolwork you'll miss. You can decide with Pari and your mother what duties must also be made up with them. Once you have these details together, you will let me know your plan. If I find it acceptable, you're free to go."

The next day, I sorted out all the details and reported them to Father at dinner. He gave his permission to go. The generosity of Mother and Pari reminded me of the respect we shared between us that was not weakened by our differences. My teacher, however, did not spare me any breaks with missed work. Clearly, he saw no value in going off into the forest for two weeks when I should be at school. "You have responsibilities to your schoolwork as well, young lady," he stated with his stern look. "I expect there will be no compromise in the quality of your work."

He could not even imagine what I would witness and learn in the forest, nor could I for that matter. I thought Himmat would be upset because he was not going, but he was content with his life as it was. Pari and Himmat had little interest in spending time with Nani and Auntie, and in extended stays in the forest.

I was advised of the essentials necessary, which were minimal. Even our food would be gotten from the forest. The two weeks of preparation passed very quickly. Early in the morning before sunrise, the three of us piled into a bus that would take us to our point of entry into the forest. We passed endless small villages.

Initially, the road was very busy with many types of vehicles from other villages. Our pace was painstakingly slow, as the bus maneuvered over the road's poor pavement and made several stops, mainly for people to get on and off to trade their goods. The volume of noise increased, as people's voices competed to be heard. The road complained of its unwieldy burden through its many potholes that widened and deepened as we progressed, and the bus complained of its noisy burden through the squeal of its brakes each time it stopped.

After some time, we reached outside of the villages. The road, now cleared of most local traffic and people's loud chatter, quieted. Lifted from the heaviness this noise carried, the bus glided over a road that welcomed it with far fewer potholes. Requiring less pressure on the brakes to stop, their abrasive squeals became wispy sighs. I breathed the welcome quiet of the bus deep within my body. The sides of the bus expanded and contracted in synchrony with my breath, creating an open space for its passengers to relax in. The burdens the noise had carried, yielded to a welcome calm.

In midafternoon, we arrived where Nani and Auntie wanted to enter the forest. We passed many points of entry much closer to our village, but Nani said they liked to travel the extra distance to be where very few people went. Nani and Auntie stopped for a few moments before entering the forest, breathing its scents within them. Its lush aromas inhabiting the many textured layers of its soil and vegetation swirled around us playfully, lifting remaining tensions worn on our faces. Once we entered the forest, Nani and Auntie surprised me when they quickly moved away from an easy, established path. "We don't need paths to follow," Auntie explained. "We allow the forest to guide us. It wants us to experience its full beauty and knows where to take us to do so."

With every step taken, Nani and Auntie blended more with the essence of the plants and animals. They spoke of the richness of the colors and smells. The nature spirits danced as their beauty was appreciated. Doves, robins, crows, and larks flew excitedly around us with their playful welcome.

Nani and Auntie knew the sounds of all these birds and sang back to them, returning their welcome. I tried to imitate the bird sounds and sing my welcome too. I do not think I was doing well because Auntie told me not to concern myself with the sounds of birds right now.

"It's much more important to let all animals know you welcome them," Auntie said with a bit of humor in her voice. "They'll know you are not afraid of them and won't harm them."

My efforts to imitate the sounds of the birds stopped, and I gave my full attention to breathing the fullness of the forest fragrances deep within me. Their energies gently massaged my heart, and I softly giggled from their playful, loving touch. Gradually, the songs of the birds found their way into my heart, where they became a harmonic symphony. Notes awakened to be sung, and then rested, allowing other notes to be sung. Their wings danced with the air currents, creating vibrations that added to the music of the forest. Their vibrant colors enriched the foliage. Welcoming this beauty through my breath, it vibrated ever more deeply within me.

Nani and Auntie talked about gathering food for dinner after walking for some time. As we did so, they taught me what plants were safe and unsafe to eat. Nani told me to never pick all the plants in one place because leaving some plants assisted with new plants replacing what was taken. "Take with gratitude," Nani advised, while making sure I understood the importance of doing so. "You're blending your energy with nature's energies, so there's no need to think of giving gratitude. Nature recognizes the heart's joy. You want distance from your thoughts. Thoughts prevent your awareness from expanding within the refined dimensions of space-time that your intuitive mind exists within."

Nani found a clearing for a small fire to cook the plants and meat that would come. She had matches with her but said she would soon teach me how to start a fire with sparks from stones. "When you are in a forest, you cannot depend on supplies brought from the village to sustain you. Anything can happen to them. Plants and animals are playful. If you allow their help by nurturing your mind and body with their delicate energies, they will always assist you.

"If you feel fear of the circumstances you find yourself in, your fear will block the help nature wants to offer. Fear can be quite the mischievous rascal. It is a large, steel barrier that refuses to bend to the unknown. Its nature anticipates bad outcomes. It keeps your breath shallow and constricted with its heavy energy. The energies of the forest that require open space to breathe within, cannot be present through the density of fear."

Auntie called for me to come with her, while taking her archery set. When we reached a small clearing, she put an arrow in her bow ready to release it. When a small Indian civet entered the space, Auntie released her fingers from the arrow. The arrow followed the path of Auntie's sight to its target, and it instantly dropped to the ground. After Auntie gently placed the civet in her bag, we returned to where Nani was making a fire. I was shown how to clean and prepare the civet, and the best parts to eat. "Our bodies need protein from meat at times, but we will not need it every night," Nani said, while placing the civet carefully in the fire's glowing flames. The fire welcomed it, enclosing its flames around it.

Our meal was the most incredible meal I ever ate. My taste buds burst from the flavors of the food. It was as if the nature spirits were experiencing the taste of what they provided through my senses before their life energies were ingested to nourish my body. In every morsel, I smelled and tasted the layered textures of the Earth's soil that nurtured the plants, and which now nurtured me through them. When we finished, the extra food was put a distance from where we would sleep. We made our beds in a clearing and fell into sleep.

I was becoming an expert at gathering food, inheriting the canvas bag for that purpose. I did not need to search for food. I learned to recognize a certain glow in the plants, indicating they were being offered as food. The boundary that once separated me from the animals and plants was dissolving. The songs of the birds became my songs. There was no need to try to imitate them. The wind inviting the plants to share its rhythmic sway became the rhythmic sway of my inbreath and outbreath. The pulse of the water's flow within streams became the pulse of my blood's flow within my body. My feet often spontaneously skipped with joy, expressing the lightness my body embraced.

Besides the birds, there were endless animal voices I was learning to differentiate. Most times, the voices blended to deepen the beauty of the forest's harmonic symphony. In the early morning and later evening, I often heard lions. Their voices, carrying both courage and fear, stood apart from the harmonic music. Listening intently to their sounds, I was reminded of Lord Shiva who was recognized for his great courage. He had yet, however, to face the ultimate test of his courage because he had not embraced the roots of his darkness through compassion.

One afternoon, as we rested on a cliff at a higher elevation of the forest, eagles circled close to us. Nani's gaze locked into an eagle's gaze, followed by a spiraling light that expanded slightly from Nani's body to enter the eagle's body. Another eagle circled around me, beckoning me to do the same. Auntie sensed my initial doubt and reassured me. "This merging with the eagle's awareness is no different than blending your awareness with other plants and animals, although it is far more intense. The eagle circling wants you to enter this union knowing you can end it when you wish. I will remain here in my body, and Nani will assist you in the sky if you choose to play with the eagle. Simply expand your breath inward to receive what this eagle wants to share."

I closed my eyes, breathing deeply to blend my awareness with the eagle. While I remained aware of my body sitting next to Auntie, I was also aware of my expansion through my breath. My chest almost exploded, opening itself through my expanding awareness. Sensing a reassurance from within the eagle's light that all was well, I relaxed and surrendered to what it offered. I was no longer separate from space and time. I was unified within space-time. I was my physical body sitting still, and I was also a light body that I shared with the eagle as we flew together united in one breath. The eagle Nani merged with flew nearby, sharing the magic of the moment.

When fully melded with the eagle's light, I was spellbound. Its light not only covered the entire forest, but the space beyond the forest as well. Its expansion was without limits. My arms were powerful wings, moving gracefully within space-time. My breath was melded with the winds, supporting my ease of flight as I breathed in unity with the eagle's breath. My eyes perceived through a golden light, transforming how I knew the Earth. I s-o-a-r-e-d in freedom.

I did not want to ever leave this experience, but at some point, I sensed my adventure needed to end. The eagle's light guided me back into my body, slowly easing its light from my awareness. The eagle Nani blended with, returned to the space where her physical body rested. A spiraling light contracted slightly as it entered Nani's body, and her awareness appeared to no longer blend itself with the eagle. Sitting in silence, I felt heavy and confined within my body. Doubt of what I just experienced surfaced. Nani's voice interrupted my deepening gloom. Turning to acknowledge her voice, the playful twinkle in her eyes danced. "Such great beauty the eagles share."

Nani's contagious joy touched my heart, easing my doubt. When I shared my feelings, Nani suggested that I not think about my experience. It was best to remain only with its joy. "Your mind doubts because it cannot explain what you just experienced, Aditi. Only a joyful heart can know that what you shared with the eagle is indeed very real."

Auntie said we needed to move along. Night was coming, and we did not have food for dinner. So, we did just that.

Nani and Auntie continued to joyfully laugh throughout the evening as dinner was prepared and eaten. Sharing my joy with them continued to ease any doubt that wanted to resurface.

I recalled little of our last week in the forest. Somehow food was gathered, animals gotten for dinner, fires ignited, and our beds of forest twigs and grass assembled. The captivating, vibrant colors of the sunrises and sunsets danced with each other, erasing the boundaries of their separate identities through the unified transparency of their colors. Nature awakened its beauty within my body throughout the day and rested its beauty at night. Hours and minutes disappeared.

With time seeming to take on such a different quality, it was easier not to question my experience with the eagle. I was maturing and expanding into a knowing that when I allowed the majesty of nature to breathe within me, it became infused within my beingness. Every sense experienced the textured layers of its presence. Nature was more than my playmate; it was my teacher through its play.

As we made our way to familiar landmarks close to the bus stop throughout the day, I knew we would leave tomorrow. While sharing dinner that night, I spoke of my contentment with life. I did not have close friends with physical bodies other than Pari, but I had Nani and Auntie. "I'm so happy with life just as it is. Both of you will always have a special and honored place in it."

Nani and Auntie acknowledged my words, but I could see their doubt. "Your mind's powers of reasoning are evolving," Nani said with great compassion. "It will want to control your choices with its new powers. The heart's wisdom is an intuitive knowing that must be trusted and allowed. It knows life differently than how your mind knows life. Your mind's doubt of this wisdom will test your trust."

There were few times when I questioned the wisdom of Nani and Auntie, but this was one of those times. "How could my mind possibly become an obstacle in my life?" I thought, while falling into a deep sleep.

Seven

Although we never met others in the forest, I knew we were not the only people there. It was not unusual for seekers of enlightenment to live in the forest. Recognized as ascetics, they avoided people and their conversation, staying a distance from them. Many once lived in ashrams, which offered a place to focus on their spiritual practice of abstinence from worldly pleasures. There they were responsible for many duties, and quarrels frequently arose among them. The forest offered freedom from ashram tensions and rules.

Forest ascetics often wandered into our village to beg for food. Auntie and Nani said most had not opened their hearts to hear and see the beauty of nature. Not allowing nature to serve them, they were dependent on others to feed them. They were taught that enlightenment was attained by overcoming worldly attachments and pleasures. All their attention was given to controlling and purifying their minds and bodies through great sacrifice. They believed suffering was necessary to attain enlightenment.

"Most ascetics and spiritual seekers in our country have Gurus, or high saints," Nani once told me. "These Gurus impart spiritual knowledge to seekers through the grace they realized within. The seeker needs to be present with an open, quiet heart to receive Guru's love. Practicing rigorous self-denial, many are used to denying love for themselves, and are unable to feel Guru's grace touch their inner heart. The wounds of their human heart create thick barriers that cannot trust and allow this deeper love. Often, their wounded hearts find expression through envy and jealousy. They feed their restless minds with drama in ashrams."

When an ascetic came to our home for food, Nani invited him or her to Auntie's house for something to eat and brought me along. One time, Nani asked an ascetic if he was willing to share what he did in the forest with me. He readily agreed to do so. He spoke in much detail of his many sacrifices and austerities. His words echoed the force of the demands he made on his mind and body, and his eyes were sad and strained. The movements of his overly thin body lacked any softness. "I gave up everything that enticed the sensual pleasures of my body and mind to realize the Pure Consciousness within. It has taken great commitment and sacrifice to stay on this path of austerity. I could endure the hardships, while others could not endure such sacrifice."

As he spoke, I recalled Lord Shiva commanding the goddess Kali to find strength to be the warrior she was. Such pride Shiva took in being a strong warrior and protector, but it hid his deepest darkness from him. I felt this same pride in the ascetic as he spoke of his conquest of sensual pleasures. All he commanded of his body felt harsh. I wondered how he could allow compassion's grace to love him when he took great pride in denying himself pleasure. Perhaps I misunderstood him.

"Lord Shiva takes great pride in his ability to battle dark forces with his light," I found myself saying. "He believes he can control any darkness. Nani and Auntie shared that Shiva's pride prevents him from seeing the darkness that remains deep within him. He must surrender his pride to allow the loving compassion of his divine heart to dissolve what remains of his inner darkness. Don't you need to be tender with your mind and body to help rid them of darkness?"

His expression showed surprise and annoyance at my words. He spoke after calming his emotions. "Your Nani and Auntie teach you differently. I do not see pride as harmful to what I am seeking. I do not see Lord Shiva's pride as harmful to his efforts to control the dark either. Like Shiva, I must let my mind know that I am in control of its thoughts and emotions. My mind and body require purification to be touched by grace, and my austerities and rituals are necessary to achieve this purity."

I recognized the kindness he wanted to show toward me, but the annoyance in his voice begged the question of why I was bothering him with such nonsense. No one spoke further. His words were familiar to what I heard at my own temple. I learned to keep what Nani and Auntie shared to myself, and the ascetic reminded me of the discomfort others would have if I spoke openly about these teachings. He quickly ate his remaining bites of food. Nani offered him a new robe, he accepted it, and he bid us his blessings as he left.

Auntie assured me I did nothing wrong by asking my question. "You spoke through the voice deep within your heart. If a person is attempting to control the mind through the mind's forceful efforts, your words will not make sense. The mind and divine heart understand very differently."

Still feeling discomfort from the situation, I said I did not want to talk to other ascetics. Auntie and Nani respected my wish, but suggested I be with them to listen when an ascetic came. Most times, I was with them to listen. The conversations were limited, but there were exceptions. There was an ascetic who was so gaunt, he had little strength to walk and speak. Even eating took energy he did not have. I saw Auntie's concern for him. "Why do you deprive your body of the nourishment necessary for this great journey you are on? Nature wants to serve you on your journey by offering you its food. If you feel and appreciate its beauty, it will serve you in return."

The ascetic looked at Auntie quite perplexed. Through a weakened voice, he expressed how all creation, including nature, must be transcended to be enlightened. "I must take my awareness out of this world, while closing my senses to its pleasures. When I have complete control over my thoughts and emotions, all distractions of my mind will cease. The illusions of this world will no longer entice me. Then Truth, the Pure Consciousness that illuminates this temporary world of existence, will be realized."

Nani shared how deeply she enjoyed blending with nature's consciousness, while appreciating how it served her when she was in the forest. "I'm taken out of the seriousness and heaviness of my mind's controlling thoughts to feel my playful spirit. Enjoying this play, my mind is unaware of the grace that is transmuting its darkness. I do not want to negate and defeat my mind to escape this world. My healthy, well-nourished body assists my mind in allowing my inner grace."

Through a depleted voice, the ascetic spoke. "It's your way to appreciate nature. But I believe you are mistaken in giving nature importance to the realization of Truth. Perhaps you are confusing creation with 'That' which illuminates all of creation. I must now be on my way. You have my blessings." Watching this weakened ascetic leave the house, I knew he would soon leave his body behind. I felt relief knowing his suffering would soon be over.

Many other ascetics were fed and clothed at Auntie's home. Most followed the teachings of great austerity and sacrifice to realize Pure Consciousness. But on occasion, an ascetic came whose light playfully danced with the light beings. Auntie asked one of these ascetics when he left his family, and how long he lived in the forest. His long, thick, black hair needed some tender care, but the movements of his slim body were without stiffness. His eyes were calm, and his face gentle. His yellow robe and sandals were very worn, but clean. I heard an ease in his voice as he began to speak of his past.

"I have a deep love for my family, but I couldn't accept their ways. My father is a doctor in the city and wanted me to follow in his footsteps. His brother, a sculptor and painter, lived nearby. He is quite eccentric, unable to live by the rules and expectations of society. When my uncle attempted to do so, he had a breakdown. My father bought him a small convenience store that was somewhat isolated from the normal flow of business traffic. It was a way to save the honor of the family and look as if everything was normal.

"But things were far from normal for my uncle. In the back room of his shop, he sculpted and painted. People were hired to attend to the customers and take care of other store business. I loved watching my uncle create his art, and he taught me much. He painted and sculpted gods and goddesses different from what I had seen before and shared their meaning with me. I felt great love and peace within him. He was so different from my father, who I always felt judgement and expectation from. My father thought my uncle was crazy and attempted to limit my time there, but he could not stop my visits."

He stopped for a moment, as if to be sure there was interest in his words, then continued to share more about his struggles. He was confused with his father's wish for him to become a doctor. His intuition told him that becoming a doctor was not his calling. When he spoke to his father about his confusion, his father said intuition should never be trusted. Only reason through logic should be trusted. Becoming a doctor would bring honor to his present and future families.

His father tried to convince him how troubled his uncle was. He was irresponsible because he could not support himself. "Wanting to appease my father and act responsibly, I entered medical school two years ago," he said as sadness entered his eyes. "But as the year progressed, my heart spoke even louder to me, and I couldn't negate it. I had to leave the university, and my father's expectations behind me. I left a note to my father asking for his forgiveness. Initially, I lived in ashrams, participating in their practices. But once again, my intuition told me this is not my path. I left to live in the forest."

I found myself unexpectedly speaking to him. "I feel so much peace from you, even though you could easily be bitter and angry. Nani and Auntie taught me much about anger, and the compassion necessary not to empower it."

"I was very confused in the ashram and forest, and I did experience much anger. I questioned if my father's words carried wisdom. The forest was especially difficult because I was unfamiliar with it. I believed I suffered from some type of mental disorder to leave all that was offered to me by my family. The intuition of my heart was always present to soothe me, but I doubted it and pushed it aside. My body became gaunt, lacking in nourishment, and my mind existed in deep anguish.

"In desperation for my life, I surrendered my mental and physical suffering. I was overwhelmed by such intense light that my body could barely support its beauty. I risked trusting how this light was guiding me to be present with it. While I have awakened to this grace, my emotions continue to surface. When they do, I feel fear as a brick wall whose strong force does not allow grace to penetrate it. The playfulness of the nature spirits and light beings in the forest helps to carry me through times of being stuck in fear, but sometimes I feel too heavy to allow their play. I push them aside, while sinking deeper into fear and doubt. These times remain challenging, but they are becoming less frequent and intense."

Auntie noticed him having a little difficulty sitting as he spoke. He was shifting his posture frequently. I thought he was not used to chairs, but Auntie asked if his back or legs gave him pain.

"Recently, I do feel some pain moving through my body, especially in my lower back and legs. It doesn't cripple me, but it is unpleasant. If a doctor is in the village, he may be willing to help me."

"I am not a doctor, but we have experienced physical discomfort in our bodies as well that is not harmful," Auntie said as she looked at Nani. "The cells in your body are changing to accommodate the intensity of the refined light you are allowing and integrating. It is natural for the body to feel pain and discomfort. It is also natural for your emotions to tease you. Emotions you blocked for so long are surfacing to be released or transmuted. They will continue to tease you with fear and doubt.

"Your mind is trying to protect what it has always known itself to be. Recognize and accept its thoughts and emotions, but do not be seduced by them and empower them. Your thoughts are not You as spirit. Nourish your mind and body by breathing love within them. Its light will slowly transmute their fears and concerns. If you want to see a doctor, I can assist you."

As the ascetic sipped his chai, his eyes closed. It seemed he was dozing, except his arm moved to sip his chai. His deep state of relaxation was contagious, and I relaxed more. I closed my eyes, fully receiving the nourishment the chai offered. After some time, I heard the ascetic take a deep breath and begin to speak through our shared silence. "I'll give your suggestions time. If I think I need a doctor in the future, I'll return to accept your assistance."

I surprised myself, as I began to share my adventures in the forest and my great love for it. I also shared my love for Nani and Auntie. "I don't know if I could feel peace if I left and was unable to see them again. I would also cause pain to my father and taint his honor if I left. Do you think your father has forgiven you for leaving?"

"When I wrote that letter, I believed it was my duty to bring honor to myself and my family. I suffered much guilt and shame for not fulfilling my duty. I now know a love that is not the love I shared with my father. That love was with expectation and judgment. If my father suffers from my actions, it is because he is not free of the limitations in how he loves himself and others. It is not my responsibility to own what he chooses to understand and experience. Nor is it his responsibility to dictate my destiny to me. A relationship that has control or power over the other carries only pain and suffering."

Auntie and Nani were silent as we spoke. When I turned

my eyes away from his, Nani went to get him clothes and money for sandals. Nani's face glowed with appreciation for what he shared as she handed him his gifts. She spoke so softly to him that I could not hear her words. He smiled while nodding slightly, as if to answer a yes, and left.

Eight

With the passing of time, I increasingly recognized changes in my mind. Not so long ago, I could not understand how people were so distracted by it. Now, I was increasingly aware of my own distraction with my mind's thoughts and emotions. Slowly, seamlessly, I was pushing aside the free-flowing presence of my playful spirit. My intuition that once spoke the tongue of spirit and nature, and my experiences of seeing, hearing, tasting, and smelling nature's textured layers were becoming increasingly foreign to me. My mind's capacity to reason through its powers of logic boasted of its potential to unveil the deepest mysteries of life. It assured me of my foolishness to believe and trust anything known through my intuition.

In school, I read the work of revered scientists in biology whose beliefs completely contradicted what Nani and Auntie had taught me. These scientists knew nature without a conscious awareness, making the science of logic responsible for controlling and harnessing it. I learned of people and events that shaped histories, and I analyzed cause and effect relationships to define reasons why things happened as they did. The past, present, and possible future of time were what defined reality and its laws. The laws of mankind served me in doing my duties in a way that earned honor and respect in the eyes of others. How could Auntie and Nani be correct, and the entire remaining population be incorrect?

When I ventured into the forest with Nani and Auntie, my trust in what they shared was restored. Away from others and their world of logic, I could be in the space of my heart to experience the world through its eyes. But once out of the forest, and back in a world where beliefs of the mind dominated and demanded conformity to, confusion again festered within me.

I felt little inspiration to paint and write. My aim was increasingly less precise when I practiced shooting arrows. It was difficult to find space from my distracted thoughts. They were a forceful noise, demanding my attention. Nani and Auntie witnessed changes in me but did not address them. I understood they wanted me to initiate a conversation about these changes, but I never did. I visited less, choosing to spend time with new friends who spoke the tongue of the mind and its accepted truths. Our conversations helped to ground and validate worldly truths. I did my best to ignore nudges from deep within me to question these beliefs.

Shortly after I turned 14, I was having a better day where I did not feel my stomach moaning in discomfort from my confusion. I heard my heart's wish to have chai with Nani and Auntie and acted on its wish. They welcomed my visit, not addressing my absence. Auntie's compassionate eyes soothed my festering emotions. The playful twinkle in Nani's eyes magically pierced through my developing seriousness. Their compassion touched those parts of my beingness that remained willing to receive it. These moments together restored me, even if only for a day.

I laughed with them as Auntie shared a story about the many unsuccessful attempts of a mother dove to coax her chicks out of their nest to fly. "You can never force one to take flight," Auntie said to finish her story. "Choosing freedom from beliefs that choke the realization of profound potentials within is never a choice made by others."

I sighed, acknowledging my understanding that my heart's compassion, not my mind's force, was necessary to realize freedom from beliefs that limited potentials of great beauty within me. Most times, I did not see the light beings, but on those very rare occasions when I relaxed my mind into my heart's vision, they were present to me. Their joyful play soothed me, just as the lighthearted presence of Nani and Auntie soothed me. Nani reminded me that she and Auntie were going into the forest in a week and asked if I wanted to go with them. I nodded a yes, feeling relieved to have distance from a world that was so confusing.

The time needed to prepare a year ago when I made my first trip into the forest was no longer needed. I could pack overnight. I knew what was expected of me from my teachers and family. I appreciated having extra work to do before going to the forest because my mind did not have the luxury of mulling over its confusion.

A couple of nights prior to leaving, I had an astonishing dream. I was standing tall in the forest, very close to a pond full of lotuses. While admiring them, a serpent glided out of the pond. It was covered in lotuses that melded into its skin as it inched toward my feet. Watching the lotuses of the serpent's skin radiate the light and dark of Kali's lotus, my initial fright left me.

An eagle flew over my head, circling above me. In front of me, the serpent moved its body upward as the eagle descended to meet it. I watched in awe as they gracefully united and became a magnificent dragon. It was as if the serpent had swallowed all space-time in its merging with the eagle. The dragon's pure, black eyes radiated a compassion that gave perfection to all that is, as it is. Its wings glistened with beams of golden light, extending far into the universe and beyond space-time as I knew it to be. Its serpent body was a translucent, crystalline light radiating through the lotuses of its skin.

Through a serene smile, its mouth parted. "Hello, Aditi," it said in a voice that held the depths of the universe within it. Vibrant waves of color flowed to me from its spoken words, enveloping my body. In that moment, I was united with an essence greater than who I knew myself to be. It was a presence unmatched by my unification with the eagle.

"I am an ally to the deepest essence of who You are. Your soul wants to merge and unite with you to create deep beauty on this Earth. You are confused about what Truth is, and you doubt the wisdom of Its compassionate love. The beliefs of the world that confuse you are the laws and values of mankind. If you accept them as your truth, you will never evolve your fullest potential. You will never experience the true magic of life. You must let go of your doubts of what Truth is, and who You are."

In silence, its compassionate eyes peered into my eyes. Drawing me into its eyes, it continued. "Do not resist the challenges ahead of you. Do not douse the potential to realize this great beauty by giving doubt power. The light deep within your heart will never misguide you. Accept the dark through your heart's compassionate light. I am with you, assisting you as you allow me to do so. Only when all darkness within you is resolved, will you reflect the brilliance of your deepest essence." As its wings lifted into the beams of light that gave them form, its compassionate eyes withdrew from me.

I awoke, feeling a profound sense of peace. My inspiration to paint returned. Finding my sketch book, I began to draw my majestic dragon. I wanted to capture its majesty in my painting. Aside from a very rough sketch, my painting needed to wait until I returned from the forest.

The two days after my dream passed quickly as I did what was necessary at home and school to complete my responsibilities before leaving for the forest. Nani and Auntie commented on my peaceful presence, but they did not probe further. I wanted to share my dragon with them in the forest. It held the magic of my dream, and it was best to wait until we were together there.

Once in the forest, I was surprised to find them take the same path we took during our first trip a year ago. We always ventured to different parts of the forest. "Why are we taking the same path as last year?"

"I believe the forest would like us to slow down and play more this time," Nani replied as she set a slower pace. "You experienced the places most harmonious with its changing seasons, which was necessary last year."

We were all quiet the first two days, shedding restlessness from the demands of the past week. Nani and Auntie felt responsible for getting ahead on sewing orders to avoid making things more difficult for my parents in their absence. I saw their tiredness on the bus, as they dozed on and off, despite the excessive noise. Recognizing my own tiredness, I often fell in and out of a light sleep as well. As the noise and activity about me arose and subsided in my dozing, I recalled how this heaviness once stressed me. Now it was a part of me. Even the squeal of the brakes was familiar to the tone in many voices I related to every day. Wearing the heaviness of my thoughts and emotions, I was without the lightness of my spirit's joy I once embodied.

Nani often lingered behind. Recalling the forest wanted us to play during this visit, I was not concerned about her. Nani was a Master of play, and I attributed her slow pace to embracing play. If Auntie and I got too far ahead, we stopped to wait for Nani to catch up. As Auntie and I sat waiting for Nani one day, the birds suddenly began to chirp loudly and flew in circles as if to welcome someone. I thought Nani was nearby. Startling me, I heard the deep, hollowed-out voice of my dragon speak through Auntie, "Hello Aditi. Such a beautiful day to share with nature."

Auntie stood up. Waves of colorful light that were of my dragon's voice enveloped us. Auntie's body became barely visible as my dragon infused its pure light within her bodily form. Its translucent light formed wings on each side of her. A serpent form, barely distinguishable from the light in her body, took shape inside it. She became my dragon. In the unmistakable voice of my dragon, Auntie again spoke, "We need to turn back on the path to find Nani now."

Auntie took the lead. Spellbound, I forced my body to stand. My dragon lifted its vibrant wings ever so delicately into the light beams surrounding it as Auntie began to walk. The rest of its body followed, exemplifying the effortless beauty of its grace. Slowly, Auntie's physical body revealed itself. I grew accustomed to magical play as a normal part of being with Nani and Auntie. It was abnormal to be with them and not witness magic. "Tonight," I told myself, "I will speak of my dragon."

We soon met Nani on the path. She was busy gathering plants for dinner. It was a bit cool as we began to prepare dinner, so we built a small fire to sit around as we ate. After dinner, I described my dream dragon, and how it became Auntie as best I could. Auntie nodded her head now and then as I spoke, acknowledging the accuracy of my description. I asked why the dragon came to me now.

"Your mind needed to mature to gain your autonomous identity," Auntie responded. "If you allow and integrate the grace of your soul's spirit, your creations will radiate Its passion and magic on this Earth. Your mind will work in partnership with Its intuitive wisdom by giving it physical form. You know there are great challenges ahead as you allow and integrate the grace of your soul's spirit. Your mind will not trust It. It will create doubt and fear to prevent you from blending your energies with Its essence."

"Do you remember that the serpent part of the dragon is a symbol of the transmuting powers of wisdom?" Nani asked.

I nodded a yes.

"The serpent slowly and methodically devours conditioned beliefs and their charged emotions that limit us. As it cleanses our body, the light and the dark make themselves known to us with increasing intensity. We accept the light as a part of us, but the dark becomes a monster we do not want to accept. We want to soar above our darkness, just as the eagle soars above the physical body of the Earth. We project onto others, what we refuse to own. But if we embrace our layers of darkness with compassion as they arise again and again, we increasingly witness the perfection in the dance between the light and the dark."

"I felt my dragon's splendor that could melt the emotions of any person willing to embrace it. Everything was perfect, just as it was. Its wings were so elegant and vibrant. Beams of golden light flowed into its wings. Where were these light beams coming from?"

"Such great wisdom your dragon revealed to you, Aditi," Nani responded as her eyes danced with their playfulness. "Maybe tomorrow we will share the story of creation. It's too late to do so tonight."

She and Auntie went to their beds, but I remained by the fire to appreciate its golden glow for a short time longer. It was the glow of Auntie's lamp at the table we always sat at to share chai. The light gracefully yielded to the dark as I slowly doused the fire with water. I naively believed that any challenges ahead would be minor and easily overcome.

Nine

The following day, I saw we were approaching the incline to the cliff where the eagles resided. Nani said she would wait at its base for Auntie and me.

"Nani, are you feeling well?" I asked in a concerned voice.

"I am well, but I am feeling some fatigue and want to rest for a while. You and Auntie go ahead."

"She is fine, Aditi," Auntie assured me as we continued. "Nani's body is getting older and appreciates more rest than it used to. There is no need for concern. Allow nature to be as it is. It is teaching Nani not to push herself as she once did. Nani is embracing this change and appreciating the gifts it offers her."

The eagles were waiting for us at the top of the cliff, and neither of us hesitated to accept their invitation to play. This was the first time Auntie and I flew together with the eagles. Auntie flew with a compassionate surrender to nature's elements that supported her flight. The eagle, used to the strength its intense light held, began to yield to Auntie's compassion that invited surrender to it. It played with the movement of its wings as if to wish them synchronized with the vibration of Auntie's radiance. It slowed the speed of its flight often, surrendering its flight more and more into the currents of air that lifted it.

When it was time to return to our bodies, Auntie's eagle expressed gratitude for what was shared, circling above her as we began to make our way back to Nani. A short distance later, Auntie looked up at the eagle and smiled as it left. I was a witness to how great strength readily yields to the compassion of a divine heart. I had yet to embody Auntie's great depth of love. I could not share with the eagle what was not yet present within me.

We walked in silence. The doubt I knew the first time I flew as the eagle was a faint whisper that was losing much of its force. When I allowed myself to blend with nature, I experienced its magic. But I did question if the magic I knew in the forest had a place in my village life. These two worlds seemed complete opposites of the other. Would conflict between these two worlds continue to plague me, robbing me of any contentment? Recalling my eagerness to hear the story of creation, I thought Auntie may be willing to share it as we walked. It would distract me from my foreboding sense of gloom. "Auntie, could you tell me a little of creation's story now?"

Auntie continued walking for a few minutes before responding. "I'll share a short and simplified version of creation's story. There Exists the Eternal, Pure Consciousness that all beings once Existed as. It is the Oneness of Source that knows no beginning and no end. Its Awareness is a sublime grace that is free of creation's polarizing energy. Through a passion to know Its own Self, Source gave birth to light beings. It set these beings of light free to create in whatever way they chose, without judgment, while remaining connected to them through Its grace. As reflections of Its own Self, the light beings would provide Source with a deeper knowing of who It is.

"However, many unforeseen challenges surfaced with the birth of creation's energy. When these light beings separated from their Oneness, they forgot their original Home of grace. For the first time, separation and the duality of opposites were experienced, creating fear. Not knowing what was missing to feel complete, they sought energy from each other in the form of power and control to ease their discomfort. Their actions led to battles between the forces of light and dark. These battles grew in their intensity on the galactic level, long before biological forms were created.

"Eventually, a rare light being understood the futility of battle. A knowingness of something greater than who it knew itself to be surfaced and deepened, as the grace of Consciousness was felt. By allowing Its compassionate grace, this being could acknowledge and accept its own darkness, rather than misplacing it onto others. Love dissolved fear, creating space for the inner lotus to bloom. When all control fueled by fear was surrendered to grace, the Truth of Beingness was unveiled. A Being realized in Truth was called the Eternal Self. The Eternal Self then created souled beings to share the same gift It was given by Source.

"Your soul, or Intuitive Self, is a creation of your Eternal Self that is of grace. Your human mind and its personality are an expression of your Intuitive Self that are with the density of duality. Your soul has a deep passion to unite with you to share your experiences on Earth, but the duality you assumed needs resolution. Grace readily flows to you to assist you, but you must allow it. Only through grace, can you embrace your inner darkness with compassion. Your dragon is helping prepare you to integrate the potent presence of your Intuitive Self and Eternal Self by transmuting your biology. The more you release fear and doubt through compassion, as you acknowledge their energy within you, the more your dragon can serve you.

"When the light of your soul's grace is fully integrated, you Exist as the multi-dimensional being that is your human self, Intuitive Self, and Eternal Self. While each is its own sovereign One, all are connected, and support the other, through the grace of Consciousness. You are the embodiment of the sacred triangle that creates through the magic of the true magician."

"What will become of who I am right now? Will all my memories leave me?"

"Your memories will remain, but they will be without their emotional charge that fears and judges. You will know a love for your own Self that the mind is incapable of experiencing without grace. You will not want to stay limited by identifying your beingness as your life story on Earth only. Freed of attachments to your history, you love all equally. Fully enveloped in grace, there is no longer a need to take or receive energy from any life form outside of your own beingness. Grace brings what is necessary in the moment.

"Creation is a love story. It is a story of Consciousness setting parts of Itself free as souls to create through Its passion of grace. It is a story that embraces the depths of our shadow through the compassion of love. You have already awakened into this grace. I believe one day you will fully realize this grace as your Truth and know that you are so much more than your mind and body. Only then will you truly realize the Truth of what I speak."

"The love in my dragon's eyes felt infinite. I want to know this love, not the love between two married people."

"The deepest love shared in a marriage is a reenactment of creation's love story. It is a love where two people are so realized in grace that battles for power and control are nonexistent. Be careful what you desire to create. Great beauty will be lost to you if you choose to diminish this potential in your life."

Lost in my longing to know this love, I almost tripped over Nani where she sat waiting for us.

Auntie surprised me the next day when she said it was time for her to meet the person to give the supplies to. She would be gone for three days. A couple of days before we left, Nani said that each of us would carry extra supplies for someone in the forest, so I needed to limit my personal supplies. When Nani and I handed Auntie the supplies from our packs, Auntie gave us things from her pack. As she disappeared into the forest, I felt concern for her safety. Nani must have seen my concern because she told me not to worry. "Auntie knows the forest well. No harm will come to her."

As we finished cleaning up from breakfast, Nani said she wanted to show me a cluster of caves. "The next time we come during the monsoon season, we may stay there."

"Does Auntie know where she can find us?"

"I am aware of where she is, and she is aware of where we are," Nani responded. I assumed Nani and Auntie cleared their plans with each other before Auntie left.

We reached the caves by early evening. They were larger than the caves we stayed in during last year's monsoons, but they did not look like they would offer any more comfort. I was unsure if I would join them during the monsoons this year. The constant rain, humidity, and stifling heat weighed me down. I often gave more attention to my personal discomfort than I did the forest.

Nani and Auntie were lost to the sounds of the forest life, especially the mating lions during this season. Their joy in what the forest offered, far exceeded any physical discomfort they may have experienced. They appreciated the rain, listening to it fall onto the Earth and watching how the vegetation opened to receive and absorb its droplets. Their skin stayed drier than mine as if they were the vegetation of the forest, gratefully absorbing the rain's ceaseless drops of moisture into their cells.

I could not ignore the contrast between what I chose to

experience, and what Nani and Auntie chose to experience, during the monsoon season. As Nani was not fully awake in the photo with Dadi, I was not fully awake to beauty when I allowed such distractions. It was challenging to ignore my physical discomfort, just as it was challenging to trust my intuition to guide me when in the village.

Nani's voice brought my attention back to the forest. "Auntie said she'll need an extra day before meeting us. We will collect some twigs to put in the caves. If we don't return to use them, someone else will appreciate having dry twigs."

I wondered if I heard Nani correctly. "Nani, I think you said Auntie will need another day before meeting us. How could you possibly know that?"

"Aditi, there is still much for you to realize about how the divine heart communicates. My Intuitive Self is not bound within a distinct point of space and time and limited by it. The universe is within me as my soul. I can call the attention of Auntie's soul to me, just as Auntie can call my soul's attention to her. When I feel her light, I speak through the light of my soul's spirit, and Auntie receives my message from the same space within her.

"There is great clarity in this communication because it is without emotions that confuse what's spoken and heard. If Auntie or I allowed doubt or fear when communicating, we would no longer be present in our hearts. Our messages would be confused by the static of our mind's charged thoughts. True clarity is shared only through the heart's wisdom. It's without the masks of who our minds think we are, and the other to be."

I nodded my acknowledgment of her words. I understood why I experienced light dancing in their shared communication and in the tone of their voices. The beauty of the space I shared with the eagle and my dragon vividly returned. I was unified within space-time; I was not separate and outside of space and time. Nani was correct. So much more became possible when I allowed a presence that is not contained within the limitations of space and time as my mind knows them to be.

Auntie showed up at the time and place Nani said we would meet her. Until the fullness of my inner depths was unveiled to me, I was without the recognition of the depth of wisdom Nani and Auntie embodied. Recognizing my deep desire to be that Master, I committed myself to the expansion of my beingness deep within the depths of my divine heart. My love for, and trust in Auntie, Nani, and my dragon felt unshakable. I would no longer allow any teachings contrary to their magic influence me. I had kept my worlds separate before, and I could keep them separate now. I would "fit in" at school by accepting their ways to know and create reality when there, but I would remain true to the teachings of Nani and Auntie. I felt so clear, so confident of my path in life. I breathed in relief for what I believed was a resolution to the conflicting views of my two worlds.

Ten

When I returned to the village, my dragon beckoned me to paint it. I asked Nani and Auntie if they objected to me having chai as I worked. There were no objections. I recognized how they willingly gave of their time to help me when they did not stay at the table long. I lost myself and the teachings at school to my dragon's magic. It felt natural to allow my dragon's presence within me to direct my strokes and choices of paint color. I did not realize that as I painted, my dragon was cleansing the cells of my mind and body of their confused chatter. My spirit was better able to breathe Its wisdom through me. Its light was becoming the dominant presence in how I perceived and created my reality. I had little interest in the conversations of my friends, avoiding them when possible.

A couple of months after returning from the forest, I was in school listening to the teacher talk about a tsunami in another part of India that happened a week ago, causing many deaths. He spoke of nature's destructive forces, and our inability to control nature. He was upset and angry because he had friends who died in the event. I saw the teacher's fear grow through the hardened gaze of his eyes and the rigid gestures of his body, while speaking of possible destructive events that could happen in our village. There was a light surrounding him that wanted to touch his heart, but his fear held this light at a distance.

The teacher's tension rippled out to touch others, creating questions filled with fear. The walls of the room moved inward as its open space contracted into a compressed space. The light of the room dimmed into darkness. The constricted energy of the room choked my breath, and it looked for an open space to expand its light within it. The heaviness of the space devoured the minds of others with its fear. I felt great concern this fear would call to those embracing it, exactly what they believed themselves victim to. Before I knew what was happening, I stood to speak.

"Sir. Please excuse my interruption. There is a light with great wisdom near you. This light wants to help you release your fear and anger, but you must open your heart to receive its wisdom."

When my voice stopped, I heard a silence of stunned minds being released from their trance of fear. Some nervous giggling broke the silence, which grew in its volume and intensity. I realized what I had done, and how it was being received. I wanted to make myself small, become invisible if possible. My legs buckled under me, feeling the panic of my mind. I forced them to find strength. Before the teacher could speak, I ran out of the classroom and home to the safety of my own bedroom. I cried and cried, releasing the energy strangling my breath through my tears.

Nani was the only one home. She knocked on my door asking permission to enter. I told her to go away. She returned a short time later with chai and my favorite treat. I again told her to go away. I continued to cry. I heard Nani leave the house. Soon, she returned with my mother and Auntie, who spoke softly among themselves until they were close to my room.

Mother began to speak gently through my closed door. "Aditi, your teacher called to tell me about an event at school that upset you. None of us, including your teacher, are upset or angry with you. Your teacher said he was a little confused about your words, but also shared he felt deep grief for those who died in the disaster. He was unaware of how his grief was creating fear in himself and others."

"My classmates were giggling at me. I was so humiliated. I agreed not to speak of the light beings I saw, but I could not silence its presence. I will not return to school."

Mother continued to speak through my closed door. "After you left, the teacher addressed the inappropriate behavior of those giggling. He shared that we all see the world differently, and different views should not be condemned. He gave a warning that if anyone participated in gossip or bullying, they would be reprimanded."

I was surprised by how well the teacher handled the situation. We were taught to respect our teachers, but this teacher now earned my respect. He was a kind man, but I knew the limitations of kindness within the human heart.

It was always vulnerable to feeling its opposite. I slowly stopped the flow of my tears. "I'd appreciate some chai, but please leave it at my door. I need space to myself." They did as I asked. Mother later brought dinner to my room and left it outside my door when I ignored her call to come to dinner.

I exposed a part of myself I had kept hidden and felt vulnerable in doing so. My strength and clarity left me, as my confusion returned, creating emotional pain previously unknown to me. My mind sensed my vulnerability, insisting that Auntie and Nani were foolish. It demanded I recognize my dragon as a fantasy of my overly active imagination. I accepted its thoughts and its demanding tone. My dragon knew confusion was part of my inner journey and was without judgement of my doubt. It would continue to dissolve my fear and doubt that would sustain their existence within the cells of my mind and body for as long as I empowered my thoughts and emotions.

My parents let me stay home for a couple of days to recover. I also had the weekend that followed. When I joined them for dinner on Thursday, they attempted to act as they always did, but I recognized an uneasiness in Father and Himmat that expressed their confusion. Father was much more skilled at hiding his discomfort than Himmat. Father said Nani had work at Auntie's house and would stay with her for a couple of days. I nodded to acknowledge his words, but knew Nani was giving me space. I was confused, but I still loved Nani and appreciated her act of love. It pained me to need space from her and Auntie.

No chores were demanded of me until Monday, but on

Saturday, I did most of my chores in silence. My teacher sent a note home with Himmat on Friday assuring me all would be well at school when I returned. Fortunately, everyone was distracted by the sudden opportunity to win a new bike in an essay contest for the upper grades when I returned. Having an old bike was a status symbol in our village, so the possibility of owning a new bike excited everyone. The topic was, "What Strength Means and How I Express It." We were told that physical and mental force should not be considered in its meaning. Most chose to enter the contest, but I declined to do so. Right now, I was unsure of what strength meant. I once believed that strength was surrender to the grace of compassion. However, I was now questioning if such an idea was complete insanity to believe.

The regard my teacher expressed toward me, as well as everyone's interest in the essay contest, made my transition back to school easier than anticipated. My friends moved on to their drama that accompanies the life of a 14-year-old. But it was my inner changes that offered the greatest assistance to my return, and to easing the merciless emotional pain of my confusion. Auntie's humiliation was far worse. Something similar could happen to me if I continued to give truth to my imagination. While I attempted to keep these two worlds separate, their differences made my choice unbearable. My integrity was a shattered piece of glass strewn on the floor that wounded me when I stepped upon its shards.

Perhaps because of my humiliation and fear of even greater humiliation, I gave my allegiance to the truth of the great majority: the truth of mankind's laws known to the mind. In my determination to stay true to worldly beliefs, I defined necessary steps to take. I would accept the teachings at school without question. I would not allow myself to acknowledge light beings or nature spirits as real. I would not visit Auntie's house. I would not allow myself to feel the loving presence of Nani and Auntie and be nurtured by it. At all times, when in their presence, I would avoid eye contact.

As the days wore on, it was clear Nani's heart understood and accepted my wishes. Her body, embodying a spirit of great wisdom, stayed a distance from me. She was respecting my needed space. Nani even changed her seat at the table as discreetly as possible, moving further away where eye contact was easy to avoid. My dragon painting was unattended at Auntie's house and within my heart. I would not allow myself to believe it was real.

I lived with my mind's fear of possible consequences for accepting as real, the magic that once gave me great joy. No one questioned me about not visiting my past magical castle. On rare occasions, when Himmat shared a topic that interested me during dinner, I chimed in with my own intellectual insights. I was "fitting in" with what was considered as normal. I refused to acknowledge any inner currents of conflict with the teachings I wanted to give my allegiance to.

I kept myself distracted from any doubt of my choice through constant activity. I lost myself to my studies at school. As worldly teachings and their energies increasingly defined and dominated my reality, my trust in what Nani and Auntie shared dwindled to a faint flame in a dying fire. The wall that separated my intuition from my logic grew in its strength with each passing day.

With my mind seizing control in its perceived victory over my heart, its thoughts commanded my attention. I wondered if my intuition was real at all. Was this childish play where my mind got lost within a world of fantasy, a figment of my mind's imagination? Is realization just a game of the ascetics who want to flee a world they could not find purpose to, and happiness in? Were Nani and Auntie existing in a shared insanity that Auntie seduced Nani into, and who once seduced me into? Was I once lost to insanity?

I attempted to ignore the changes I saw in Nani's body in my occasional glances her way. Her playful, carefree movements full of ceaseless energy were yielding to movements more precise in their execution. A part of me wanted to talk to her about this change. But if I opened myself to share intimacy with her, I would falter in my effort to keep distance between us. I comforted my concerns by holding onto Auntie's words in the forest that Nani is merely slowing down due to her age.

When I was especially tired, I felt the wisdom of my heart calling me. But I would not allow myself to answer its calling. I was sure I could move through all my confusion if I continued to give myself space from Nani and Auntie and their teachings. I did not realize that while I attempted to silence the voice of my heart, on a deep, inner level of knowingness I could not deny its Truth.

I often visited Auntie's archery range knowing I could trust her to leave me alone. The focused center I had almost perfected was lost to my distraction. I saw only the distance that my mind measured and calculated to determine when it was best to release the arrow from my bow. Lost to the sight of my heart, my aim was no longer what it once was.

Eleven

By the time I turned 15, Pari was married for nearly a year and living at her husband's home. On occasion, Pari and her husband came to visit, but we had little time to talk together alone. During her most recent visit, Father asked Pari to share some duties of her married life with me. Though she expressed much contentment through her voice and eyes, I could not share her contentment. Pure dread was in my belly, which I attempted to keep hidden from my sister. When Pari left, Father and Mother sat with me to talk. "It is time," Father began in his firm, but loving voice, "that we begin the process of finding the man you are to marry. It is your duty you must accept as a young woman." Mother sat beside Father, acknowledging his words with a nod of agreement. Her eyes, in contrast to Father's eyes, did not meet mine.

I froze, lost in a deep panic at the thought of living a life I could not identify with. "Please, Father," I instantly retorted through my panicked voice, "I am not yet ready to marry.

I do not believe I ever want to marry. My duty is to this household now that Pari is gone. How will Mother manage without my help?"

"Aditi, your duty is to your future husband and children. Most likely, you will not marry for a couple of years, as you are still young. But it is necessary to start the process of finding the proper husband for you. Commitments must be given, and the necessary arrangements begin to prepare you to live with your in-laws, and them to live with you.

"Your brother is also getting close to the age of marriage, and his wife will live here to assume many of your duties when you do marry. I will hire the help necessary to sustain this household if needed. It is the accepted way of life that women in our village assume." Any attempts to argue with Father would get me nowhere. Desperate for help, I went to protest to Nani and Auntie seeking the nurturance I had been denying myself.

They welcomed me with their warm, loving smiles as I entered the house carrying with me the turbulent, swirling energy of an uncontrolled tornado. In her usual calm and collected manner, Nani put her arm within mine, while embracing my hand. I felt her slow, steady breath. I attempted to breathe her breath within me as she calmly guided me to my familiar chair at the table. Sitting, the chair felt to support me with its own calm, while welcoming my return. I had never noticed the warm comfort my chair held. But neither Nani's breath, nor the comfort of my chair, could subdue my panic. It deeply gripped every part of my beingness. Rather than breathing the slow, deep, calm breath of Nani, I breathed the fast, shallow, chaotic breath of the tornado I entered with.

Auntie and Nani listened intently as I shared my story through a voice that hurled itself outward toward them with its panicked intensity. Both remained calm, unaffected by the energy I flung toward them. The compassion worn on their faces found a space within my tightness that soothed my body and mind. I was able to find enough calm to end what had become idle chatter.

"We knew that soon this duty would be placed before you," Nani said through her soothing voice. "We cannot assist you in changing your father's mind. It is not our place to do so. You are a woman now, and you need to decide your own options and choose which of those options you will act on. Auntie and I will support you as we can with your decisions, but we will not try to persuade you or your parents to act in any way. Ask your heart for guidance and decide your options and choices accordingly. We have done our best to prepare you for this decisive moment."

My difficulty not reacting to my swirling emotions showed itself in its full colors at that moment. When Nani and Auntie saw my eyes tear, the expression on my face contort into anger and frustration, and my mouth open to voice my objections, they quickly left. In doing so, they spared me the humiliation of witnessing my outburst that followed. I angrily cursed all those I knew through screams that only Auntie's magical castle could find tolerance for. My screams turned to sobs until my body could no longer support the trauma of my upset. When I calmed down a bit, Nani and Auntie returned and made some chai. After they put my favorite biscuits on the table next to my chai, we drank in a welcomed silence. It soothed my shattered nerves, and I wondered if they put a special herb in it to help calm my upset.

Auntie began to speak about my destiny. Feeling calmer, I was able to open my heart to receive the compassion her voice and eyes offered me. "We have given you the freedom to make your own choices. Understand that in doing so, you assume full responsibility for the destiny that will follow from them. Nani and I see your potential to allow and integrate the wisdom of your Intuitive Self and Eternal Self within your physical body. It is your choice how deeply into your heart you expand to do so. If you choose to fully allow the grace of your divine heart to guide you, your commitment to this work needs to be above the respect of family and friends. You can no longer attempt to 'fit in' with the world others have created as their reality.

"We recognized your attempts to accept the teachings at school and those around you as your truth. We also recognized, however, that you could not fully negate your intuitive knowing of a greater Truth within. Your ceaseless involvement with worldly activities, and related thoughts and tensions of your mind, kept you distracted from the stillness and quiet your heart requires to be heard. But there were times of quiet when you were present in your intuition without being aware of its guidance."

Auntie's voice yielded to silence. The quiet of the silence encouraged me to go deeper within my heart as calm increasingly replaced panic. My breath was expanding, opening space within my cells to feed them light. I breathed compassion within my mind and body, while exhaling my panicked energy from them. After giving me time, Nani began to talk softly. Her voice blended with the resonance of the quiet, assisting the expansion of my breath even deeper into the space that was opening to receive the calm wisdom of her voice.

"The confusion you know between your intuitive Truth, and worldly truth, is fragmenting you. You are in a void that cannot provide a sense of stability any longer. You must make it very clear to both your Intuitive Self, and human self, which one you will honor as your master. If you choose to venture into your inner depths, the wisdom unveiled there will guide you. Your mind will assume its new role as a partner to your soul's spirit, but it will never be the master of your Truth.

"If you choose to make your mind the master of your truth, then lovingly release the support of your spirit. It will accept your decision without judgement. Your expansion inward through Its wisdom will be halted. As Its presence slowly leaves, you will be increasingly guided by the beliefs of man. Your inner knowing through wisdom will become a faint memory. Like the minds of most adults, it will accept what you experienced as childhood fantasy if the magic of your intuition surfaces at times.

"You will be a strong and beautiful woman regardless of your choice, but you must decide the type of strength and beauty you want to resonate in this lifetime. Know that the path of wisdom will demand far greater strength from you. You will encounter the depths of creation's light and dark within you to transcend both. This journey will require a steadfast courage to trust a knowingness that is not of this human world. It is time to summon, through a calm and focused center, the energies necessary to support you on the path of your choice. Perhaps an opening will present itself to choose differently in the future, but the hardships created by this change will be far greater."

I nodded, still sniffling as I savored the comfort of the tea and the softness of their presence I so deeply loved. I showed so little regard for their grace for a long time. "You have given me only love and support, but I doubted your words and avoided you. Yet, you show no resentment or bitterness for my behavior. I feel only your compassion. Please understand my confusion between what you teach, and what the world teaches. I do not know what truth is anymore. I do not know the path of my destiny."

After encouraging me to drink my chai and waiting for me to do so, Nani spoke. "Our love has always been constant, regardless of your pleasure or distaste for us. We know who You truly are, even though you have yet to discover this. Give yourself a couple of days to define your options and decide which one is best for you. Stay clear in what is of your inner heart, and what is of your mind. When you decide which path you choose, you are welcome to share it with us if you want to. If we can help without interfering with what must be your responsibility, we will do so.

"You must not delay your decision. Your father's anger

will be more difficult to temper if he has begun the process of arranging for your husband, and you choose to go against his wish for you to marry. He does not like the family's honor humiliated by failure to follow through on his word to others."

Again, I nodded that I understood. We finished our chai, and I left to spend the night alone. Their strength and compassion pierced my heart as I left. In their own unique way, they would help me to see the path of my greatest potential.

I sobbed that night as I pondered the pros and cons of my choices. Initially, I thought there was no other choice than to accept the wishes of my father. Why did I feel marriage so dreadful anyway? Pari and Mother were content in their roles, so why couldn't I find contentment as a wife and mother as well? Father would not pick a man with a cruel and unjust nature. Perhaps a love I had begun to feel absent within could be rekindled in my relationship with a husband.

But my heart would not find peace with this choice. Instead, it felt tight and constricted, objecting to this possibility. I remembered Auntie's words about the boy she once thought she loved, and of the limitations of love through the human heart. I remembered how the love between Nani and Dadi changed into something of greater beauty after his passing because they freed each other of their emotional bonds through the human heart. I remembered how Auntie spoke of the love that is the reenactment of creation's story, which required that each partner be realized in the love that is of grace. Father would not find me such a person, nor had I realized this grace. But what other choice could there be?

Running away to another village would not help. Others were suspicious of a woman my age who was alone. I would be an outcast begging each day for food, while living on the streets. Only an ascetic of the forest would not be questioned if alone because aloneness is the nature of the ascetic's life. Perhaps Nani and Auntie knew what was ahead and taught me how to live in the forest to have an option for marriage.

I experienced what it was like to give my mind authority. As the outer world of my mind and its logic gained influence over me, I did know a level of activity not known before. My activity was with an agenda that sought recognition and honor from others through my achievements. It reinforced the constant chatter of my mind's reasoning because it did not honor the quiet ways of my intuition. The emotional charge that accompanied my thoughts smothered any faint glimpses of quiet. I knew little peace, just as those I attempted to "fit in" with lacked true peace. I acknowledged the emptiness that bled within my organs when I attempted to deny the magic I once knew.

Taking a mirror to my eyes, I saw they carried sadness too. These were not the eyes I perceived through when I trusted my intuition. But was I being a responsible adult to believe my intuition was real? Wasn't my mind serving as a necessary guide to teach me what is necessary as a responsible and honorable member of my community? Isn't it my duty as a mature adult to assume the accepted beliefs and roles of my community, while earning the honor of others through my contributions to better my community?

My confusion of what was real, and what was fantasy, was overwhelming me. I laid down from my exhaustion, while surrendering my pounding head to the softness of my pillow. I felt a beautiful energy within my space and began to breathe in its soothing essence. Soon, I was sound asleep.

Time loses its presence in sleep, and my mind's powers of reasoning that depended upon time to exist were no longer present. Without its beliefs of what is real and unreal, the magic of my soul's spirit was freed to reveal Itself. I became aware of two golden eagles filling my room with their blazing light. Looking into their eyes, I knew Nani and Auntie had blended their energies with these eagles. I breathed their vibrant, pulsating breath deep within, creating space in the cavities of my body to be filled with their light. I was soon lifted from my room and onto a forest cliff.

It was the same cliff where an eagle once shared its awareness with me. This eagle returned to me, and I accepted its invitation to join its flight. Nani and Auntie, still present as eagles, departed. My wings stretched themselves into their full span as my breath fully merged with the winds that carried my flight. Through the eagle's golden vision, I saw the many light beings and nature spirits living within the forest. My joy seeing them again was deep. Happy to see me acknowledge their presence once again, the joy they returned magnified my own joy. I questioned how I could have ever doubted them as real.

A young woman at the outer edge of the forest came into my vision. Much light surrounded her, but she was unaware of this light. Her fear did not allow her to notice the light wanting to dance with her. Recognizing my own fearful and self-critical mind, I knew this girl was me. I feared for my future, believing I was irresponsible to risk the safety of the known, especially to follow a path that may hold only the fantasies of a childish imagination. The possibility that I was seduced by Auntie to believe in this fantasy made my self-critical thoughts scream, "Do not act like a fool any longer to believe what Auntie and Nani say. Follow the safe, known path of marriage. You will find happiness there. You have much to contribute to your community."

With my vision now surrendered to the eagle's vision, I lovingly accepted my fears and thoughts as they were, but I did not want to accept the choice dictated by the fears my thoughts were charged with. I saw a beauty dormant within me that could be awakened if I willingly disempowered my commanding fears. I saw myself full of joy, enjoying the deep beauty that life is. Feeling the calling to return to my body, I brought my awareness back into my room.

Twelve

The sun's early morning rays fell upon my face as if the golden light of the eagle wished to waken me. Even though awake in this physical world, the events of my dream and its deep beauty remained awake within me. But as I slowly blended with my familiar surroundings, the dense beliefs and emotions of my mind began to flow within my blood. Doubt seized the opportunity to reassert how foolish I was to believe what I experienced in my dream as real. After all, it was just a dream. "Leave me," I sternly told my doubt. "I claim my dream's beauty as my Truth, and I am willing to risk anything to claim this wisdom." The energies of the forest summoned me during my dream, comforting me with the knowing that they would serve me if I allowed them to. I knew what must be done.

Desiring to feel my arms as wings that lifted me out of the fear that wanted to weigh me down with its heaviness, I floated into the kitchen where Nani already began to prepare breakfast. Looking into my eyes, she knew my choice. "Come talk to Auntie and me when your chores are done. We will tell you how we can assist you to live in the forest." I opened my heart fully to receive her nurturance. As it calmed me, the pain I tried to quell when I denied my heart's intuition surfaced.

The rising sun captured my attention, inviting me to be present in the potentials it offered to each new day. Nani stood by my side, assisting my breath from getting stuck in the wounded emotions of my human heart. "The intense distress of pain carries great potential," Nani said softly. "When embraced as a teacher, it can propel us on an inner journey to unveil a space of immense love where emotions no longer have the power to affect us. Joy is our Truth, not pain. We suffer from pain only because we have forgotten our Truth and do not allow Its expression within our beingness."

Nani and Auntie were all business when I came to see them that afternoon. Nani was assisting Auntie with putting sewing items away. "When do you think you will be ready to leave for the forest?" Nani asked before I sat at the table. We did not even make chai yet.

I gathered any strength I could mobilize, wanting them to recognize my courage to follow a destiny of great risk, but of equally great potential. In a firm voice that surprised even myself, I shared that it was best to leave early the following morning. "Procrastination will not serve anyone's interest. Time would give fear the opportunity to stop me. It would hurt to keep my secret from my family. I prepared a list of what I need." They nodded in agreement as I handed Nani my list.

Nani added to my list, while giving advice. "We already began putting things together for you and can easily finish packing today. I will pack two yellow robes and other items that will fit into a backpack. Do not put the robes on until you reach the forest. Someone may recognize you, and you want to avoid any attention. There will be food for your lunch and dinner, but then you must depend on the forest to nourish you. I will speak to your father at breakfast tomorrow. He will be angry initially, but in time he will accept your choice. He recognizes your wisdom, even though he is unable to understand it and help you evolve into it.

"You have the knowledge of the forest necessary to take care of your needs and safety. Your heart will protect you if you allow its presence and surrender to it. You have witnessed the joy of the light beings and nature spirits who will serve you as you reawaken into your intuition. Remember, fear has power only if you choose to give it power. Be present in compassion. Stay alert to choices made through your divine heart, and choices made through your human heart. Observe the difference in how you feel, and what you create from those choices. Be the wise woman you have already started to become."

I was now willing to accept the isolation necessary to realize my freedom. I was grateful I would not remain in the village as Auntie did. I would travel deep into the forest where others did not travel. Perhaps an occasional ascetic, but they kept to themselves and hidden from others.

"There are villages deep in the forest. You will find both men and women there who are much like Nani and me,"

Auntie said as if to hear my thoughts. "When you enter these villages, they will provide for your needs. There will be times when your mind tries to seduce you into doubt of what you have chosen. If you weaken your resolve, visit these people. They will not preach to you. Their presence will help restore your strength through clarity."

We all became silent, lost to our anticipation of what was to come. Nani's voice entered the silence seamlessly as if speaking through it. Her voice carried the unobstructed wisdom of the silent depths it arose from, just as the colors of the sunrise carried the transparency of the sublime depths they arose from. "I want to finish putting together the necessary items for your journey." She slowly stood, and like a feather, floated away.

I would miss the beauty in the voices and eyes of Nani and Auntie. I wondered if my own voice could bring calm to me in challenging moments ahead. I experienced Kali's sense of resignation when she chose to go within, rather than to join Lord Shiva to battle dark forces through her light. Everything was at risk, including my own identity and security as I knew them to be.

Auntie suggested I help get chai and biscuits together, while Nani continued gathering my things. While making the chai, I asked Auntie how long I would live in the forest. The thought that I may never be with them again weighed me down.

"Most likely, there will be great changes in you, and there may or may not be a desire to return here. Focus on the fullness of the present, while expanding into the depths of all that can be experienced within. Never force your future. Allow the lotus of your heart to unfold it for you."

Auntie put an herb next to my chai. I knew the herb was helpful for restful sleep and decided to add some to it. All necessary arrangements were spoken of. Silence again filled our space as we savored the last moments of our time together. When the last drop of chai was sipped, I stood, and they did the same. Sharing hugs, their clarity moved through my mind and body, easing my distress of leaving them behind.

"You will find your pack on the porch in the early morning," Nani said as strongly as her strength allowed her to. "Catch the first bus leaving, which will have only one or two people from this village going to work. If they ask questions, tell them your father asked you to deliver the supplies you are carrying. They will get off the bus in the next village and not know your destination. You have a beautiful heart that is yours to claim. Go within. The beauty you find there will give you strength and guidance. We have set you free. Now you must set yourself free."

Feeling deep sadness in my parting from them, I closed the door behind me. I was also closing the door to who I was, and all I was attached to as that person. It was time to leave life as I knew it behind me and walk on into my Truth. Trusting Nani and Auntie to take care of any remaining details of my leave, I fell into a deep sleep as soon as my head reached my soft pillow.

Thirteen

I awoke before sunrise from a light knock that I thought I heard on my door, but no one was there when I opened it. Becoming aware of what was to occur today, my sleepiness was quickly jolted from me. Before the sun rose, I was out of the house. I found my backpack exactly where Nani said it would be. Money for the trip was on top of it. My archery set stuck out, but no one would question me about it. Many people carried one when traveling. The lamp on the table where we always shared chai was on. Auntie had already started her sewing. The glow of its light reached out through the windows offering its soothing golden rays.

Fear's voice attempted to seduce me into choosing the safety of the known. I numbed myself to not feel anything. I did not want to live the consequences of being entrapped by fear's wishes. My decision was made when I was of the eagle's clarity. If I empowered my fear, all clarity would leave me. My feet would freeze in their tracks. "Keep moving to the bus with my feet and into my heart with my breath," I said

with resolve. "Fear, I will not sink into your crippling grasp."
As I left the property, I felt Auntie and Nani encouraging
me on with their blessings. Fear's heaviness began to lift its
presence, although it hovered over me with its readiness to
conquer my resolve, should it weaken.

Winter's harshness was softening its presence, and I did
not need to cope with its extreme cold. It would be a couple
of months before the summer's intense heat would arrive. "A
perfect time to begin my journey," I told my fear, letting it
know that all was very well.

There were only two people from my village on the bus,
just as Nani said. They ignored me, dead to their routines
of the day. At the next stop, a woman who knew me asked
if I needed help. I told her I had very explicit instructions
where my father wanted clothes delivered and needed no
help. Nodding approval, she left the bus.

As time passed, the noise and activity escalated. Its
swirling, unfocused energy fueled the endless concerns of my
mind. Were my parents able to accept my decision? Would
father be angry at Nani for knowing of my plan and allowing
me to follow it? I recalled the words of the ascetic who shared
that his father did not own the responsibility for his destiny
as we sat at the table that supported Auntie's lamp. Even in
daylight when not supplied with an electric current, her lamp
glowed with the sun's radiant light. Breathing the warmth of
its glow within me, I soon fell into a peaceful sleep.

A light streaming through the bus window woke me
shortly before my stop. Everything came back to me, but I
refused to be coerced into panic. I welcomed the sun's warmth

and the quiet of the bus that now carried few passengers. I opened my pack to find my lunch right on top. There was no need to disturb other items. Auntie even put chai in a small flask. The aroma and flavors of my chai and favorite foods lifted my panic, just as the rays of the sun lifted an early morning fog.

I got up to leave when the bus arrived at my stop. The driver looked at me with concern. "There is only the forest here Miss. Are you sure this is your stop? Are you lost?"

Nani forgot to advise me how to handle suspicion from the driver. I had to respond calmly and wisely to avoid trouble. I opened my pack just a little, so he could see the yellow robes on top. "Thank you for your concern. My father is a tailor who makes robes for ascetics. A couple of times a year the robes are delivered to them. The same ascetic knows when and where they will be delivered and will soon arrive to pick them up. I asked my father to bring the robes this time. I want to spend a day in the forest with the ascetic. I will take a bus back tomorrow. All is well."

"Such a gorgeous day to venture into the forest. Enjoy every moment." After paying him, I got off the bus, and it slowly began to leave.

As the bus pulled away, it created a vacuum of space from my village life. It was the moment fear had waited for to strike, filling this void with its demand to end my foolishness by taking the next bus back. Its intensity was magnified by remaining tensions from the bus ride. I stood still, taking deep breaths. "Go forward, not behind. This journey is an adventure," I assured myself. The vibrant forest presence entered me, calming me with its inner silence that it arose from, and rested within. Breathing its serenity deep within, I massaged my fear with its calming light. Approaching the great kingdom of the forest, I asked that it welcome me with its magic.

The sun's afternoon rays glowed through the dim shadows of the forest's winter foliage. I smiled as the image of Kali's playful lotus revealed itself. She was present in the forest as well. She would not protect me, but she would assist me in moving out of my belief that forces existed outside of me that I needed to protect myself from, and battle with. If I allowed the grace Kali radiated, she would help me embrace my inner darkness.

In a gesture of accepting her assistance, I joyfully laughed at her play. Nani and Auntie were given a house to embrace their inner darkness, and I was given the forest to do the same. They were excited for a house where they could integrate their divine heart, and I chose to feel that same excitement with the forest. With each step taken, the welcoming dance of the forest's magical play revealed itself more. The birds playing around me lightened each step taken.

I started to walk toward a familiar path and then stopped. Nani and Auntie never entered the forest with a path already chosen. They allowed the forest to guide their steps. Wondering if I was still able to blend and merge with the forest's magical light to receive its guidance, I found a clearing a bit removed from the path to relax in. Sitting down,

I felt my fatigue. Dark was coming in a couple of hours, and I decided this was a good place to spend the night. Everything I needed to make a comfortable bed was within the clearing. Nani's words to take with gratitude in the heart helped me ease within that space as I gathered twigs and arranged them into a comfortable bed.

Resting on my bed, I looked in my pack. The robes reminded me that I should leave my old clothing behind in the morning. "One last night sleeping in them," I thought with hesitation, "then I will assume my new identity as an ascetic." I had to keep digging in my bag for my dinner, which Nani placed on the bottom. She wanted me to see the two small paintings she and Auntie gifted me. They were wrapped in a black, silk cloth with golden threads woven throughout it. Nani's painting was a much smaller image of her painting of the goddess Kali standing on her coiled serpent. I had yet to befriend the compassionate grace of the serpent and was vulnerable to fear. But I took a very important step to do so.

The painting by Auntie inspired me in a different way. It was an image of me next to a lion. My eyes were vacant as if to question what essence would illuminate them. The lion's eyes radiated the compassion I so loved in Auntie's eyes. An eagle, with its wings fully extended over the lion and me, was almost lost to the dark cloud it was painted within. I stared at this painting for some time, wanting to reach into the depths of the message it held. "Presence within my soul's spirit is needed for my wings to take flight," I thought. "The time will come my beautiful mind, when you will see that what is offered to you is worthy of your trust and partnership with It." I carefully wrapped my gifts in the elegant softness of the silk cloth and returned them to my pack.

I took my dinner out. I had similar food for lunch on the bus, but now the energy of the food mixed with the energy of the forest. The familiar sensation of my taste buds exploding with joy returned. I laughed as I welcomed the nature spirits to enjoy the food with me. I digested not only the food, but also the light energy that created my food. Its energy tingled throughout my body as I digested it. When my food and chai were finished, and the containers cleaned, I welcomed the energies of the forest into my sleep. Listening to the sounds of the forest sing me a lullaby, I peacefully entered sleep.

In a dream, the figure of the goddess Kali stood before me in a forest setting illuminated in pure, white light. She was as Nani painted her, but she held only the lotus with the light and the dark throughout it in her hands. Next to Kali stood a massive lion, much larger than what was found in our forest. Its deep, black eyes radiated a compassion exactly like the eyes of the lion in Auntie's painting. I sensed a shared vision between the lion and Kali. Neither sought control or power over the other. Absent of creation's opposing forces within them, they were full in the completeness of the grace they embodied. This grace danced between them, just as it did between Nani and Auntie.

I was amazed at how Kali had tamed this lion. Through the compassion she radiated, it was evident she had embraced all her inner darkness, and its need to do battle. Her warrior energy was absent. The lion, the transmuted consciousness of her mind and body, now willingly served the grace she embodied. It understood its role as a respected and honored partner to Kali's creations.

"Would you like to tame your lion? But I warn you that there are great risks, including the possible loss of your life." How different Kali's voice was from when I witnessed her telling Lord Shiva to leave her. It now held the quiet strength of compassion.

In awe of such an offer, I readily responded, "Yes." I found my body in a hospital setting receiving a blood transfusion. Something went wrong as I received this blood, and I knew my body may not endure the procedure. I surrendered to its outcome. It seemed only moments later when I awoke in my body hearing the forest's early morning sounds sing to me. I shed my sleepiness, as if to shed the worries I carried. Finding a stream to wash in, I invited the playful presence of the nature spirits. They had not left me. In my mind's refusal to acknowledge them as real, my vision veiled them from me. I celebrated reuniting with them.

After washing, I put on my yellow robe and buried the clothes of my former identity. I offered any resistance from my emotions to the Earth, while asking it to transmute any doubt. I embraced the fullness of what this moment offered. Finding an abundance of plants that I could eat without preparing a fire, I ate my breakfast. Nani packed some matches, but I wanted to use them sparingly. I would start my fires using sparks from rocks when possible. I savored what was left to the luxuries I knew. Even more, I savored the love of the person who packed the matches.

Sunrises and sunsets embraced each other as I increasingly surrendered into the magical light of the forest, losing all sense of time. The light beings became more vivid each day. I was welcoming back the magic of my heart and playing within it. I had no worries. I allowed the forest to serve me and never lacked what my body needed. During the spring, I traveled as far into the forest as my strength allowed me. The coming heat of the summer would be intense, and I wanted to be in the densest vegetation for protection from the heat.

Lions also sought the protection of the dense vegetation to cope with the heat of summer. Occasionally, we caught a glimpse of each other. They sometimes came closer out of curiosity, but there was always a cautious distance between us. I often felt the presence of Kali's tamed lion as a spirit friend that playfully teased me about my fear. Unlike Kali, it was not yet possible for me to know fearlessness. It showed itself if I tried to force too much light, too soon. "I must remember not to force anything," I reminded myself, recalling Auntie's words to allow my inner lotus to unfold from within. "No wonder Auntie spoke those words to me. Force seems to create distance from grace."

Nani and Auntie lived within the magic of the grace they embodied. They taught me about magic by allowing me to witness the creations of grace through them. My dragon, the eagle, and all of nature continued to teach me the ways of magic. Magic required a gentle strength from within to choose the clarity of grace, and the patience for this clarity to mature. Trickery of the mind had no place in this magic. The mind was with its own illusion of separation from its soul's spirit. Creating from a space of limitation, deception was necessary to make others believe their magic was real. True magic was the manifestation of the grace of Consciousness into physical form. All was possible as a fully integrated, multi-dimensional being. Props and deception were unreal within this sacred triangle of beingness.

Most days, I surrendered more deeply into the playful knowing of nature and its magic. I was trusting and welcoming a deeper layer of reality. The deepening colors of the forest foliage enticed me to perceive ever deeper into their transparency. The symphony of the animal sounds challenged me to find the space within that could accommodate the depthless tones of their voices. The various signals the plants expressed when offering themselves as my meal, heightened my vision to see them. There were times when I experienced so much joy, I believed my challenges were behind me, and I was free.

Toward summer's end, however, thoughts surfaced that suggested all was not well. It had been an exceptionally gruesome, boiling-hot summer. I began to feel cooked by the heat, and relief from the sun's merciless, searing rays grew in importance each day. When the vegetation cracked under my feet as the sun's rays sizzled on both of us one day, the rawness of my burnt nerves snapped as well. My mind recognized the perfection of the moment to express its woes. "Are you totally crazy?" it demanded in a gruff voice. "Do you really believe what you are doing here in the forest has value? Aren't you running away from life and its responsibilities?

Why can't you see that you allowed yourself to be misled? Suffering is a natural part of the human experience. It is nonsense to believe you can be free of it. Look at how you suffer right now."

It seemed that when I started to feel heavy and weighed down by these thoughts, birds would appear to tempt me into play with them. Most times, I allowed their playful presence, but there were times when I lost my strength to be with clarity and told them to leave me. During those times, fear had its way with me. The animal sounds that once created a symphony of beauty were engulfed by the dominating voices of the lions. Their voices resonated fear as if to remind me that my fear was very real. Believing more danger was on my path than assistance, I was more alert to serpents and other poisonous animals on my path. But those times of turbulence eventually subsided because I found space from them to allow the compassion that could ease their force.

Fourteen

The monsoon season arrived with a full roar. I was not welcoming of it. I sought comfort in the coolness of empty caves to escape the continual downpours and overbearing humidity, but their darkness eroded any comfort I sought. The blackness of their dark space seeped inside me, arousing the deep roots of my inner darkness. My strength to get distance from my stormy emotions was waning quickly. Memories of comfort in my village, and my choice to give that comfort up, relentlessly taunted me. Feeling irritable by my doubt and growing fear for my future, I was less receptive to the play of the nature spirits and birds. I ignored them, and the light beings I had welcomed back into my life. My former thoughts of Auntie being a trickster and a seducer emerged.

I needed new clothes and the comforts of a village to soothe me. "Perhaps the change will help to renew my strength and lessen my doubts," I thought with an effort to distract my mind. I recalled Nani's words about seeking the presence of the village people should my doubts and fears begin to overwhelm me. Admitting my need for help, I left the shelter of the caves to find a village. The downpours were relentless, just as my heavy thoughts were relentless as I pressed my feet forward. The squeaks in my sandals that were unable to support their moisture, mirrored the heaviness in my steps that were unable to support the burdens I began to assume.

My anticipation of being among humans stirred memories of those I left behind. My sadness and unwillingness to acknowledge any magic the forest offered increased. With time more present in my awareness, worries of how long it would take to find a village nagged me. Every step became a chore to endure. I missed my brother's annoying dinner talk, my sister's talk of her married life, and the daily reminders from my parents to get things done. Most of all, I missed Nani and Auntie, even though I was unsure if I could trust their words.

The tense, relentless drone of my thoughts was amplified by anxiety about being in a village. This was the first time I would be with others, while assuming the identity of an ascetic. Would I be questioned? Was I truly safe even when wearing the yellow robes? I felt guilt and shame for problems I believed I created for my family, especially Father. I attempted to relax my mind, but the force of my fear was too demanding of my attention to gain space from it. It constricted my heart's vision, making present only those feelings of love not freed of expectation and condition.

Finally, a small village revealed itself in a small forest clearing, and I entered with much apprehension. It had less than 10 small cottages and was completely still. "These people must be of the forest who do not need civilization to support their daily needs," I thought, relieved that everything was so simple and quiet. I saw no one, but a woman about Auntie's age approached who came out of nowhere. She asked if I was hungry and wanted food. Avoiding her eyes, but feeling compassion in her voice, I nodded a yes and followed her.

Her simple home was full of the elegance of pure light. With a graceful movement of her hand, her thin finger pointed to a chair for me to sit on. Her tiny frame turned to prepare the food. She gave her full attention to it, carefully cutting and mixing it, while softly singing enchanting, melodic songs I never heard before. I slowly relaxed in her presence, releasing much tension as I did so. My tumultuous emotions were surrendering to the calm her mesmerizing melodies gave voice to.

I savored the simple, but generous meal she placed before me. I slowly digested each delicately prepared bite, nourishing my body with the grace she infused into my food. She honored my unspoken need to avoid eye contact, occupying her hands with sewing as she continued softly singing soothing melodies. Their vibrations pierced the depthless chambers of my divine heart, while dissolving the heaviness of my doubt.

"I'm glad to see you nurture and care for your body by allowing the forest to serve you," she said as she refilled my cup with chai.

Her words held the lightness of the words spoken by Nani and Auntie. Tears filled my eyes as the comfort of her voice touched the space my mind's doubts could not touch. "Yes. I was taught well by very wise women who were my Nani and Auntie in my village. Your voice and mannerisms remind me of my love for them, and my pain of their absence."

"They are absent to you on a physical level only. They played with you in the forest through the various forms they assumed, and you played with them when you allowed it. You found me to remind you that they are not absent from you if you stay aware in light, where their presence can be felt in other physical forms. You know that within the light of creation, is also the potential for its dark. Stay aware of what you are choosing to empower."

Our eyes met for the first time, and I saw she understood the heaviness of the burdens I carried. "If you choose to suffer, the suffering will define you. It once defined me. Fear and doubt live within you, as parasites live in a host; they maintain their life by feeding off your energy. Wisdom does not suffer from the discord of your mind's emotions. Breathe the sacred, hollow breath of your soul's spirit deep within. Through Its compassionate light, the conflicting polarity of your emotions will yield to an inner calm of quiet."

Her eyes radiated great clarity as she spoke, and I was captivated by them. Peering deeply within them, I saw golden spirals that touched my inner turbulence with their deep acceptance of it. Without hesitation, any swirling emotions that remained, ceded to the calm of her love. Dizziness came over me, and I was grateful for the chair I sat on. She placed water on the table for me, then turned to fill a small container with food and a flask with chai. She excused herself to gather clothing in the other room.

Returning, she handed me everything I needed for warmth and comfort. A beautiful shawl, just like Mother would make, was on top. Her graceful finger pointed to an archery set in the corner. She asked if I would like to replace what I had with a new set. When I nodded my acceptance, she placed it on the table with the other items. I carefully put the treasures in my backpack. When I turned to leave, the door was open, and she was gone. I saw no trace of her as I returned to the forest.

I reentered the forest, replenished in mind, body, and spirit. It was puzzling how she knew so much of me. Like Nani and Auntie, she handled my emotions with deep wisdom and compassion. As a witness to the graceful elegance of another true Master, I yearned to realize her depth of wisdom and compassion within me, just as I yearned to realize the inner depths of this beauty within Nani and Auntie.

My days passed far more peacefully as I returned to my play with nature. The melodic songs of the wise woman remained with me, soothing me in moments when I was teased with distracting thoughts. The rains of the monsoons were yielding to the cooler temperatures of the winter. The cooled forest dampness that the sun had not yet absorbed, began to ache within my bones. My body's pain suggested rest. I needed stillness to hear the melodic vibrations that my own divine heart sang.

A couple of days later, I saw a small cliff I could extend outward with twigs and grass for a home. After spending time in the darkness of the caves, I wanted sunlight passing through my dwelling to warm it and assist my spirits from fading into the dark forces of my mind. There was a deep stream a distance away with vibrant vegetation along its path. This path offered plenty of food and distance from my living area to clean animals if needed.

When my home was ready, the exhaustion of my body set in. I was ready for nights of deep sleep, and days of minimal walking. I looked forward to a fire every night to warm me. I relaxed into what became a routine of self-care. The paintings from Nani and Auntie remained at the side of my grass bed. I often recognized their presence in an occasional bird as it danced around me, inviting me to play. The birds never stayed long. They assured me that I was never alone and reminded me to play. My shawl, always draped around me at day and used as a blanket at night, provided comfort to my physical and emotional needs.

In many ways, my relationship with my shawl reflected my relationship with my mother. She nurtured my physical needs, but she could not nurture the needs of my soul. Recalling a memory where Mother told me to go to Nani for an answer to a question I asked, I understood Mother knew some of my needs were beyond what she could provide for. She saw in me what she saw in her sister and mother. She loved and accepted me in the same way she loved and accepted Auntie and Nani. I could treasure what she was able to provide for me, just as I could treasure my shawl.

I frequently heard the roar of lions nearby. I learned much about the lions in our area. Most already mated and were with cubs. Perhaps there was a pride nearby with two or three females and their cubs, as well as a couple of males to help protect their pride. Perhaps, also, there was a pack of male lions that would attack the pride, while killing or wounding the male protectors and their cubs. Although the females would fight them off, the strength of the pack usually overpowered their attempts to save their cubs. The pack would force the submission of the females to mate with them to sire their own cubs.

Most times, I trusted I was safe, but I was not freed of the depths of my fears. Sometimes, when I heard lions during the day, a chill ran through me as my body tightened with fright. Not wanting this tension to intensify, I often practiced shooting arrows. It never failed to expand my awareness out of my mind and into my heart center. I sometimes felt the presence of Auntie helping to steady my focus as my beingness expanded inward to my heart center. Believing I was now almost as skillful as Auntie, I playfully asked if she agreed. At night, after I placed my archery set at the foot of my bed, I quickly fell into a deep sleep. Lost to all activity about me, I had no concern of the lions. I trusted the forest would watch over me in my sleep.

Fifteen

The cold of the winter that gifted me with a serene hibernation was passing. My well-rested body was grateful for its time of inactivity. My sleep had been deep and peaceful, and I seldom recalled its dreams when I awoke. The energies of the forest pulsated within my blood with increasing depth. My breath was infused with the subtle breath of the forest, and my heart sang the melodies of its vibrations within the open cavities of my body. The various sounds of the large animals inhabiting the space around me, no longer aroused alertness. A part of them inhabited space within me, as our energies blended during my hibernation.

As the heat of the early spring sun warmed the damp cold of winter, the birds became more playful, prodding me out of my nest. It was time to begin my journey back into the density of the forest to better cope with the summer heat. With change in the routine I had established, fear for my future again surfaced. "Fear, you are still present, I see. Allow me to embrace you with my joy," I stated aloud. Breathing my light-filled breath deep within every fiber of my mind and body, I began to walk.

Days passed since I left my winter home. It was a little over a year since I had entered the forest. I often stopped to experience the full beauty of nature's synchronized rhythm joyfully dance within me. I could not deny its wisdom that burrowed itself within the cells of my mind and body during my hibernation. Auntie was right. Deep changes were taking place in me. I could never return to my village if it demanded that I accept their beliefs and create through them.

On a beautiful, crisp morning as I was walking, a moan caught my attention. It was the moan of a large animal, perhaps a lion. I attempted to locate where the sound came from as I walked toward it. I soon saw a wounded lion with a short, blond mane. I approached him cautiously with an arrow in my bow, should he attempt to attack me. But I very quickly saw he could not attack me. He had been viciously attacked by a pack of lions. Most likely, the cubs he sired were now dead.

I placed my arrow back into its case. I assured him, in a soothing voice, that I wanted to help. Not sensing any resistance, I placed my hand on his body assessing how badly he was hurt, and my potential to help him. The wounds were deep, but I saw no evidence of infection. I was unsure of how much blood he lost. Believing he would survive and heal, I found water nearby to wash his wounds. The containers that once held food and chai to ease my pain, were now used to ease his pain. He slowly released his tension as he increasingly surrendered to my help. I named him Zaya, which means life.

I saw Zaya's determination to heal as the first week passed. I learned from Auntie and Nani how to make healing remedies from plants to ease pain, prevent infection, and facilitate healing. Zaya never resisted what I did to his body, even though some of the remedies could burn a bit initially. I siphoned water into his mouth using leaves, and each day he was able to drink more. By the end of the third day, he was lapping water from the containers.

I was grateful for the nearby stream. Zaya's intake of water was increasing, and the containers were quite small. I saw the remedies were working well to heal his wounds by the beginning of the second week. I could relax my concern of them getting infected. His physical strength was improving, and he could walk the short distance to the stream. Lions sometimes indulged in porcupines for food, and I was able to provide that to him on occasion.

As with Zaya's need for water, his need for meat also increased. By the end of the third week, Zaya challenged himself by attempting to kill small prey. He recognized his lack of strength and speed for larger prey, and his appetite did not yet require it. While I was grateful that he could begin to care for his needs, I was concerned he was easy prey for larger animals. Zaya knew his weakness and stayed close to me. He had witnessed me killing animals for him and knew I would offer protection for his life if needed.

Zaya was well enough for me to leave him, and I wanted to move on. I was not sure whether Zaya would remain by my side as I left, but I was not surprised to find him following my footsteps. I sensed gratitude for saving his life. Zaya trusted I would not harm him, and I trusted he would not harm me. With the passing of spring, Zaya increasingly regained his health, and a very unlikely friendship had blossomed. His physical strength and speed were recovering, but not enough to support the meals he now required. One day, as he was chasing a baboon, the animal repeatedly got away. It sensed Zaya's weakened body. I decided to help Zaya with my arrow once he cornered the animal as best as his strength allowed him to. I did not want to discourage Zaya's healing and independence by making the hunt too easy for him.

Our rhythm in the hunt improved as it became a mutual game together. Zaya challenged me with my ability to keep up and aim, as much as I challenged him to regain his full strength to hunt independently. Our signals to each other improved as we jointly created and refined the best strategy for success with each kill. Zaya read the vibration of my thoughts and responded accordingly. Our communication was clear and focused, uncluttered with the human play of emotions that begged power, control, and attention in relationship with the other. "Perhaps," I thought, "I am becoming proficient in the ways of the heart to communicate, just as I had witnessed Nani and Auntie communicate with each other."

I was slowed in my journey into the denser areas of the forest by Zaya's constant need for sleep during the day, which started to wear on my contentment. I was the only one annoyed. The nature spirits used the extra rest time trying to get my attention to play. The light beings showed up at times, humoring me with my seriousness. Even Zaya ignored my annoyance when I prompted him to go on just a bit more before he rested.

Zaya's instinct was completely in tune with nature's changing seasons. He was without concerns of the future because his reality was not of the dimension that past, present, and future existed within. He would reach the density of the forest when he needed to be there. "My concern to cover more distance shows that I am with my mind's ideas of space and time. It does not want to surrender to nature's rhythm that does not abide by measured time," I admitted to the light beings one day as I accepted their humorous play. "You win, I trust we will be in thick vegetation before the worst of the heat annihilates my stamina." Taking my breath into a space that knows no minutes and hours, I went to the nearby stream to play as Zaya slept. The more I allowed nature's tempo in my play, the more my concerns flowed out of me and into the water.

With the anointing of the full intensity of summer's sweltering heat as droplets of sweat covering my skin, we were well within the density of the forest that shielded the full force of the sun's fire from us. Zaya recovered most of his strength. It was remarkable that he killed an antelope with his enormous physical strength, while also being my friend. At night, when I laid my body close to his, he playfully rolled over, while welcoming me with his soft, low moan. We appreciated the coolness of the nights that last summer's heat would not yield to.

He was most active during the twilight periods of day and night, but he aroused himself from sleep often at night. Even while sleeping, a part of him remained awake with fear for his life. A sound or scent from a possible predator jolted him to his feet as if to prepare to defend what must be defended. Allowing his fear to create fear in me, I denied myself a deep sleep too. My sensitivity to his arousals increased, and I grabbed my archery set often.

Zaya's fear of what the forest offered him dominated over trust. He trusted his physical strength only. His inner restlessness was a creation of his fear. I was allowing this fear to strip me of the deep contentment I once knew when I trusted and blended with the energies of the forest. "It is the way of instinct," I thought. "I do not believe Zaya's instinctual fears can be changed. But I have been down this path many times, and know I can, and will, move this fear out of me."

That night, I found enough space from Zaya to sleep where I would not be disturbed by his stirrings. He looked at me while pacing as if to beg the question, "Why aren't you laying down next to me?"

"I'm tired of being awakened by your restlessness and want some space for more restful sleep," I said in a somewhat irritated voice.

Unused to this space between us, and the irritation in my voice, Zaya continued to pace for a while, seeming to seek a space of comfort for himself. Watching him pace, I understood his lack of inner peace. His instinct kept him alert to forces outside of him that could harm him. Any threat required his immediate reaction to ensure safety. Zaya's knowing was of an instinctual mind. It was a mind devoid of the ability to reflect on his behavior to change it.

My surrender into the protective light the forest offered was not so easily done. In my own vulnerability to fear, I accepted Zaya's knowing that there was much to fear. It was important to stay alert, even while sleeping. Touching my archery set, I wanted to get distance from it. At the same time, I wanted to keep it by me. I heard the voices of lions that carried a fierceness to keep predators away. It was a fierceness motivated by a fear they attempted to cover. "Isn't your fear a weakness that predators recognize to gain control over you, despite the fierceness in your voices?" I called out to the lions. "Look at how restless you are from your fear. You know little peace."

The goddess Kali placed her sword at her feet when she realized the wisdom necessary to understand how the emotions of a warrior get stuck in a game of action and reaction to negative and positive forces of the mind. "I robbed myself of peace by accepting fear as real. My fear blinded me from nature's wisdom that wanted to serve me. Wow, such power I've given to my mind's fallacies!"

I took my archery set and laid it at my feet. I would no longer use it as a fierce symbol of power to protect myself from fear. Surprisingly, I experienced only minor resistance from my mind. At least for the moment, it was tired from its ceaseless battles with itself and the world. Stirred by the sound of a lion, I laughed at my instinctual reaction to grab my archery set. Catching myself, I relaxed my mind and body as I surrendered my warrior energy to the forest.

A bliss with the potential to set the forest ablaze with pure, white light enveloped me. Yielding the weight of my body to the weightlessness this blanket of light offered, I blended with it. An eagle came to me, inviting me to fly with it, and I joyfully accepted its invitation. Through the eagle's eyes, I saw Zaya sleeping peacefully now. But restful sleep was not to last for him. His fear would soon arouse him. I sensed he would soon leave to mate.

Sixteen

I spent some time blending with the eagle's presence, enjoying the great clarity of its vision in my flight. At times, I embraced Nani's playfulness. Other times, I embraced Auntie's compassionate surrender into nature's elements that supported our flight. The eagle responded to my compassion as if to acknowledge the depth of the space it radiated from. "My mind really is yielding its force to my heart's compassion," I joyfully shared with the eagle. My flight embraced the total joy of surrender. My love for Nani and Auntie teased me with visiting them, but I sensed it was not yet time. We would reunite when I was ready to do so.

Shortly before dawn, I reentered my body. When I awoke, the radiance the night held remained vividly alive within me. "Perhaps my wings were illuminated by my dragon's grace during my flight," I thought as I breathed in its magnificent serenity. "Dear dragon, your presence is welcome anytime," I said in a wishful manner to it. "Why haven't you come to me?"

"My dear Aditi. I have been waiting for you to summon me. I have always been present within you during your journey." It was my dragon's deep, resonating voice. There it stood in front of me, full in its stunning majesty. Endless beams of light illuminated all of space. "Within you, my serpent energy has been devouring the toxins of your carbon-based body and mind to prepare them to blend with the crystalline energy your soul's spirit embodies. Hovering over you, my eagle energy has been filling these cleansed spaces with light.

Most times, you have allowed this light with increasing passion to make this transmutation possible. Laying your sword down, as a symbolic gesture of surrendering your warrior energy to end all battles, was an outward act of your mind's inward surrender. Much of the energy that sought to create battle has been transmuted through grace."

I could barely focus on its bellowing words, whose vibrant colors enveloped me. My dragon was quite patient though as I breathed its magnificent splendor within. Bringing my attention to its compassionate eyes, it spoke. "I see you're ready now, Aditi, to focus on the wisdom I speak through. When you gave your allegiance to your mind and not to your divine heart, I could only speak to you through your dreams, where your eyes were closed to this physical world, and your mind's logic rested. You have allowed so much light that the subtle dimension of the dream world is now available to you, with your eyes wide open. You now understand the strengths and limitations of logic. You know You are much more than your Earthly identity and its mind."

Accepting my dragon's invitation to share its vision, a laser beam appeared that pierced my skin to see inside it. As the form of my dragon merged into this light, I followed the laser beam inside me. I saw the spiraling movement of the serpent, clockwise and counterclockwise, within my cells. The serpent's counterclockwise movement spiraled deeper into the translucent light at its center, dissolving into it. My cells were mostly of light, but some darkness remained. The clockwise movement spiraled outward, beyond the boundaries of my body's skin. While there was much light within this spiraling movement, it carried the threads of my remaining darkness.

"The clockwise movement spirals outward to give the light and the dark that remains within you, a physical form. Your body can now allow the most refined and inspired light of creation that the eagle embodies. As splendid as this light is, however, the eagle does not embrace the most profound depths of creation's darkness. It chooses to soar above it.

"The darkness remaining within your mind and body is the most resistant to change. It fuels the remaining life force of your mind as it knows itself to be. While your mind has allowed much light, it will continue to taunt you about the silliness of believing that your beingness is more than the mind when it senses weakness in your commitment. Your mind fears a partnership with your soul, whose grace will serve it as well. It does not want to give up the control it has known, even though it recognizes its suffering. You know it accepts suffering as being necessary."

The purity of my dragon's voice was without the static

of creation's oppositional forces. My Earthly identity surrendered to its magnificence, allowing my heart's expansion into the vibrations my dragon's words resonated. "Your darkness is not evil. It is compassionately gifting you with the opportunity to transcend all of creation's duality, by embracing it through grace. All of creation is with perfection when you see through the eyes of your soul's spirit. Its breath is far more vital than the breath of your mind's logic. It is a golden spiral of pure, luminous light devoid of creation's light and dark.

"The potential for you to transcend all of creation's duality is slowly lighting up. It is important that you continue to assure your mind of the important role it will assume as a partner to your Intuitive Self and Eternal Self. Only through its cooperation, can wisdom be given form on this physical plane. Honor and embrace your mind with loving compassion, but never make it your master."

My eyes, completely surrendered to my dragon's vision, were guided to the light and dark within my cells. The light beam in their middle grew to an almost explosive degree. Projecting itself to the front of my body, this beam became my dragon's form. Its translucent light was present everywhere, making its form barely distinguishable within its light. There was not an inside or outside, or any other direction to contain and limit its quasi-physical form. It was present everywhere, teasing the boundaries of my own identity. But I could not fully blend with its light.

"As an ally to the spirit of your Intuitive Self, I guard the gate to this pure light. You are aware that your mind and body must be prepared to fully integrate Its presence. In time, Aditi, I believe you will claim this light." My dragon spoke to my heart as waves of deep joy that massaged it. "When you realize this all-pervading Consciousness to Exist in partnership with your Intuitive Self and Eternal Self, you will create with utmost magic and splendor on this Earth plane. You will be the embodiment of the sacred triangle: the great magician that does not accept illusion as a Truth.

"Keep allowing the light as you embrace the dark through grace. Stay strong in compassion, while loving all parts of your beingness through it. Do not doubt your Truth. Do not become complacent with who you are now. There are far greater potentials within you to be realized." My dragon's form dissolved itself within the translucent light at its center. Space dimmed itself into the light I was familiar with.

I slowly became aware of my body that sat on my bed trembling and collapsed onto it. I breathed the dragon's presence within me, playful with the remaining darkness in my cells. I reminded myself that enlightenment required patience, maturity, and ongoing devotion to wisdom. Being with my dragon brought back the memory of its unfinished painting at Auntie's house. "I'd love to work on that painting," I said to the forest wistfully.

Zaya was unusually playful that morning, nudging me from my bed. But as the intensity of the afternoon sun waned, Zaya's playful disposition also waned. The heaviness of his fear returned as he attempted to settle into rest. I let him be. Such restlessness was his way, but I would no longer participate in making his fear my reality and reacting to it. I would do as my dragon asked. Physical and emotional distance grew between us. Each day, we grew more accepting of our aloneness as we found our food and slept. I increasingly embraced the joy each day offered to me. Zaya increasingly embraced the fear and restlessness each day offered to him.

The sun of the dry summer season was yielding to the clouds of the coming monsoon season. The discomforts this season offered started to pierce through my joy. Despite my wish to avoid entanglement with fear, it was difficult to get distance from Zaya's restlessness as my anticipation of the monsoons wore on me. One morning, when I awoke, Zaya was gone. I knew he left to mate.

Zaya was an animal of the wild, and he belonged with his own kind. We gifted each other with a new life, each in our own unique way. But a part of this new life was a co-dependency to nurture and protect the other, which I now understood as destructive to both of us. The divine heart did not give and receive love as the human heart did. It radiated an unconditional love that was without expectation and attachment. Unconcerned whether others received this radiance or not, it was clean of any emotions that included guilt, shame, and resentment. Inwardly, Zaya and I had come to exist in very different realities. We each embodied a love the other could not embrace. Our parting was an inevitable part of my change. I did not mourn this separation. I celebrated the change in me that made it necessary

I needed to leave the physical space we shared. It took a

couple of days to prepare for a time of much walking, and Zaya was often nearby. As I gave my farewells to my beautiful companion, I also gave my farewells to any warrior energy that wanted to seek its life force within the cells of my mind and body. I headed to where there was an abundance of empty caves to protect me from the rains. I was amazed with the buoyancy of my feet on the ground. The Earth became balls of cotton that gently embraced and lifted my feet as I playfully bounced on and off its surface.

The monsoon season arrived quickly and mercilessly as dark beads of water that covered me with their heaviness. The Earth's porous surface that once breathed the lightness of air became heavy with dark beads of rain that clogged its pores. These heavy droplets of moisture suffocated the lightness of the Earth's breath, just as they suffocated the lightness of my breath. The dark dampness of the caves melded into the cells of my body, and the fiber of my clothes that covered it. I knew there was little sense in a trip to the village now. "I must wait another month. If I go to a village now, everything will be ruined within a week."

The forest had served me well, but a calling from within to leave its physical space was intensifying. My mind and body wanted assurance they would be relieved of living through the discomfort of the monsoons on a yearly basis, and I did not want to negate their needs. I often attempted to blend more deeply with the vegetation to absorb the moisture into my body as I had witnessed Nani and Auntie do. But my heavy thoughts, and the discomforts of my body, would not yield to the space their magic resided within. A vision of

Auntie's lamp glowing its radiance, despite what surrounded it, came to me. Its radiance touched me, just as the radiance of Nani and Auntie touched me, regardless of the amount of physical space between us. I stopped to breathe its golden glow through my heaviness.

A handful of birds hovered above, fluttering their wings to release their wetness on me, while merrily chattering. Then they bounced on and off the Earth's surface for a short time, splashing in puddles as I laughed. They again released the moisture from their wings over me before flying away. I understood the message their joy brought. The parched Earth must yield its glory to the rain's compassionate blanket of silence. The heavy, dark beads of moisture burrowed into the Earth's foundation to cleanse it of deeply embedded decay. Once restored by the rains, the Earth will again birth majestic splendor. Nani and Auntie understood the gift the monsoons offered, drinking the compassionate droplets of moisture into their cells. Blind to their wisdom, I knew only suffering during the monsoons.

The stories of the many ascetics who visited Auntie's house became present as a tapestry of suffering and sacrifice. Such deep commitment, fortitude, and loyalty to their realization they exemplified through their acts. Their commitment was to their enlightenment, but their fortitude was sourced from a personal will that demanded their mind and body to change through rigorous daily rituals of purification. Their acts were not freed of personal will. They carried the forceful effort of a mind that assumed full responsibility for what it could not deliver.

I wished to yield any forceful effort to a love that is not of the human heart and mind. I would allow the beauty of my soul's spirit to experience Its passion through me in my daily activities. "The majesty of my divine heart *is* real," I found myself almost yelling to the forest, "and Its grace *only* can transmute the fears and doubts that still simmer within me. I will not allow doubt and fear to rule over trust and beauty. I will not allow drama to occupy and fill me with its energy. My strength is the clarity of my beingness as my human self, Intuitive Self and Eternal Self."

While I said these words with conviction, I recognized that the space I existed within at any given moment remained delicate. I needed to honor everything, just as it was, to stay away from force. With desires surfacing to return to village life, my mind wanted proof that this partnership could truly work. It knew space and time, cause and effect, and action and reaction, just as the minds of those in the village knew, and which I withdrew from. "How can a Consciousness independent of these qualities not be doubted by my mind?" I questioned aloud to the forest. "Is this partnership truly possible, where all facets of my beingness can exist at the same time when in a fear-based world that is of the mind?"

Seventeen

My acceptance of the monsoons, and appreciation for the healing powers of their darkness, greatly enhanced my ability to cope with any physical discomforts. Its darkness gifted me with being the witness to the drama my unresolved energies created. The more I embraced the cleansing rains, the less they bothered me. My discomforts did not leave me, but they did not hold the charge of emotions that created my burdens. I even practiced absorbing the droplets into my skin, but I was far from the expertise of Nani and Auntie.

The month I waited before finding a village for supplies, passed quickly. After a week of travel, the scent of comfort alerted me of my closeness to a village, even though it was not yet visible. "See my dear mind, I am taking care of you," I found myself saying. "I understand you need to earn my trust. Give me your trust, and I will give you your freedom. This partnership can work."

Reaching the village, I saw it was much the same as the previous village I had visited. Its silence was broken by a male voice coming from behind me. Turning toward his voice, I saw a young man who was not that much older than me. My eyes readily met his, which radiated gentleness and warmth. I recognized who he was. "You're the kind ascetic who visited my Auntie and Nani when I was younger," I said with excitement. He acknowledged my words with a nod, while leading me to a cottage.

I wondered how he knew I would come here and questioned him about that. Before he could answer, he led me inside a small cottage. The warmth of light filled its space that was quite empty of furniture. Abundant food and drink were on a table covered in a black silk cloth with golden threads woven throughout it. Great surprise must have shown on my face when I recognized it as the same cloth Nani wrapped my paintings in. Too stunned to say anything, I went to the table to absorb its softness.

With a gentle smile, he gestured for me to sit. Enticed by the aromas flooding my senses with desire to experience them, hunger took priority over questions. Every sense immersed itself in the pleasures the food offered. Even my hearing was stirred, expanding into the depthless chambers of my ears to listen to the melodic vibrations the food held. They sang the enchanting melodies of the village woman. All questions were forgotten.

"I see you're enjoying the food," he commented after I delicately savored over half of my meal. "The light beings at your Auntie's house came to help me prepare it. They are very pleased with what you allowed in the forest. I felt their joy as I made your meal."

I acknowledged him with a nod. My attention returned to my curiosity of how he knew I was coming to this village, and where he got the cloth. The questions that awaited their time to be voiced, spun out from me. "How did you know I was coming? Do you live in this village now? Did someone see me and alert you that I was on my way? Where did you find this cloth?"

"An eagle alerted Nani and Auntie that you'd be here within the coming month," he responded in a voice that resonated the warmth of the smile on his face. "They've always known your whereabouts, blending with the awareness of different birds to check on you. They sometimes shared the joy of their flight with me. They requested that I come here with a few things for you, and I gladly obliged their request. I left over a month ago and have been waiting for you a couple of days now."

"You have seen Nani and Auntie?" I blurted out with excitement.

"Yes, many, many times. When I was about to leave on my first visit there, your Nani told me to return as often as I liked to paint. I did not consider leaving the forest before her offer and forgot about it for well over a year. But as time passed, a weary restlessness to leave the forest was settling in. One day, as the nature spirits blended with the foliage, I sensed the forest wanted me to share its light through my paintings. I recalled the offer of your Nani. It was as if she knew there would be a need for me to paint one day.

"I decided to accept her offer. When I arrived at Auntie's house, she said you had left to live in the forest a little over two months ago and why. It was evident that she and Nani remained connected and attentive to your needs at some level. Nani told your father why I was at Auntie's and asked if I could sleep and be fed at the family house. He agreed, so long as I was willing to assist with household chores. However, he gave me very minimal chores so I could devote almost my entire day to painting. Everyone seemed content with my presence. I filled a vacant space that all were learning to accept. As I understood your father better, I knew he believed his generosity toward me would bring the family good karma."

"Auntie and Nani must have been comfortable with you to invite you. I was comfortable with you. Even the light beings liked your company. It was rare for them to enjoy playing with others. Are they well?"

"Their joy and playfulness remain, but Nani's physical strength is fading somewhat. She cannot keep the pace she once did. Auntie began going into the village to avoid burdening your Nani and mother with her needs. The priest who was at the temple left to live in a retirement home in the city six months after you left. A man close to your father's age came to run the temple. He told your Nani and Auntie he felt pulled to their village and asked to be transferred to it."

I was amazed that Auntie was going into the village. But she came into a strength that was not affected by any gossip wanting to linger. She radiated a joy that others could receive, if they chose to let go of their judgment and discomfort. "Do I have her strength not to be pulled into the doubt I knew when I left the village?" I asked myself as my gaze went inward to hear my heart's answer. "Am I really ready to leave the wise guidance of the forest?"

When I brought my attention back into the room, he was getting up from his seat to clean. Wanting to gain his attention, I realized I did not know his name and asked for it. He put what was in his hands back on the table and sat.

"I recently named myself Azad, which means free and independent. For some time, I remained nameless. When I first visited Auntie's house to paint, I felt nothing but bliss in reuniting with my artwork. But as the energies of the village slowly and seamlessly seeped into my awareness, I became confused about my choices. Perhaps my father was correct about my uncle, and what I was becoming. We were irresponsible and a burden to others.

"The shame and guilt I believed to be free of, returned with a force that tore through any sense of well-being. The light beings I once enjoyed the company of became an annoyance. My inspiration and creativity gave way to boredom and frustration. I recognized the silent love and acceptance Nani and Auntie always radiated, but my shame blocked their support. Feeling too lost to be around others, I returned to the forest. Nani, Auntie, and the light beings let me be just as I wanted. They understood without giving them an explanation. I knew I was always welcomed back."

Azad described his efforts to gain clarity to get distance from his mental anguish. "I was swept into a bottomless hole that offered no grounding or substance to my identity. It was shattered into endless pieces floating in that hole. I did not know what pieces I needed to grasp and glue together to define myself. Feeling a desperate need to just survive this anguish, I initially deferred to my father's beliefs for relief. I decided it was not too late to go back to him and apologize. He forgave others for their offenses. He would forgive me too. I would return to medical school and bring honor to him and myself."

As I listened, I recognized the same doubt and anguish I once knew. "I experienced much the same and know its pain well. Now I understand Nani's words that pain carries the potential to transcend all pain if we embrace the inner journey it propels us on."

"My anguish did become a great gift to me. Otherwise, I wouldn't be here." Azad continued to share how he headed back toward the city, traveling through the forest to do so. As he left the energies of the village behind and stopped thinking about what decision he must make, his mind relaxed into his heart's enjoyment of the forest. He became playful with the nature spirits and allowed the light beings to share more of their radiance with him.

Halfway to the city, he knew he must return to his paintings and the energy of Nani and Auntie. "I have not yet freed myself of all fear, but its force has lessened. My mind is mellowing and trusting more as it surrenders to the grace of my heart. It does not blame anyone for anything and is seldom affected by the actions of others. It more easily sees its follies when it gets pulled into drama. Its roar is a purr most times."

I laughed with him, thinking about Zaya, and missing

him. "The magic of the forest has helped me in much the same way. Lately, it has been nudging me from its protective nest. My body and mind want the comfort of home. I feel inspired to paint again. I want to return and be with Nani and Auntie, but I cannot do so if my father will not accept my ways. I cannot live by his worldly laws and values."

"Nani wants you to know she calmed the anger of your father over time. He does not understand Nani's ways, but she earned his respect many times. He would not reproach you for what was done. Your father long ago forgave your Nani. In forgiving her, he also forgave you."

"I know my mother accepted my ways having gone through so much with Auntie when they were young. But I also know she must support Father's wishes. That is the role of women in my village once married. I imagine it was difficult for Father to forgive me."

"Your father has a great heart as his name implies. He follows the rules of man and their logic, but his actions are charitable. His generous nature forgives more easily than others. There will be some discomfort as you find your way with each other once again, but I assure you his anger is no longer present. You may find distance in your relationship, but he will not force his ways on you."

Azad continued to explain that although Nani and Auntie guarded my safety in the various forms they assumed when I was in the forest, they wanted me to believe I was responsible for my own safety. Otherwise, I would seek protection from them, rather than finding the inner strength to let go of my fear that accepted limitation as real. "Never once did they have to interfere. They have such deep joy for what you have allowed. They know, however, that your strength will be tested for some time, just as their strength was once tested. Like you, I also continue to have my strength tested, but I do not find it necessary to leave the village anymore."

"Given what you said, perhaps I'm ready to return. I do not know how I will support myself though. I do not want to be dependent on anyone for my care and lack skill in sewing for Father's business to earn money."

"The village is not what you previously experienced it as. The new priest is an evolved soul, even though he is careful what he shares. When he met your Nani, he read her eyes as she did his. Nani invited him to Auntie's house where the paintings were shared. Amazed by the essence they carried, he offered to contact wealthy people from the city who would most likely be interested in buying some of them. Many of the paintings were sold at a price we never imagined. Auntie no longer sews for your father's shop. He understands she is a mystic and talented painter. He encourages her artwork now."

My face lit up as I pictured others appreciating the art Nani believed would be valued one day. "Did they have interest in any of my paintings? Were any purchased?"

"Your paintings reflect the innocence of grace a couple of buyers liked very much." He told me more about the buyers and the price paid for my paintings. "When your father saw how your paintings were valued, he shared with Nani that he was wrong to force his beliefs on you. He's freed you to follow the destiny of your choosing."

It was unimaginable that my paintings were valued by

buyers and purchased. It was even more unimaginable that my father freed me from his demands. I was becoming free, just as Azad was becoming free. For the first time, I was able to embrace my name as belonging to me.

Azad stopped talking when he saw my attention drift from his words. When I looked at him again, he continued. "The village people accepted me and Auntie when the news of the paintings became known. They see us as respectable artists, contributing to less gossip about Auntie now that she goes into the village regularly. I now live in a separate space behind Auntie's house. I do not want to live anywhere else. Auntie anticipated a visit from you at some point and added a room to her house for you. You know there is plenty of land on that property for you to build your own home. There is also plenty of money for a house."

I nodded a gleeful yes. Azad handed me a case with clothes like I once wore. I welcomed the softness of Nani and Auntie in them and wore their softness as I tenderly placed the clothes on my body.

Eighteen

As I began my return to the village, the monsoons were lifting, just as my resistance to accept the compassionate nurturance of the water droplets was lifting. Even my steps were effortlessly lifted from what was now the soft, giving surface of the Earth. The chattering of my mind was relaxing to feel peace. On those nights when it was necessary to sleep in caves, my inner heart heard their compassionate darkness lull me into sleep with their baritone vibrations.

Azad and I talked little the first two days, but by the third day a mutual comfort between us budded. Our laughter and conversation grew each day. After dinner, we shared stories of our lives and dreams. A rhythm to our daily routines emerged as we easily read from the other what was necessary to do. Enjoying his company, and the companionship of all physical and nonphysical beings within the forest, concerns of my return were absent.

Many nights, Azad shared stories about the magical ways of Nani and Auntie, and what they did over the past couple of years. Auntie's paintings were praised for their ability to reveal the magic of the forest animals. Buyers commented on how the eyes of the animals carried a wisdom they seldom saw, even in the eyes of adults. Her paintings sold almost as quickly as she painted them.

Nani continued to love her time in the kitchen cooking, even though my parents told her many times they were happy to hire someone to cook. She eventually accepted some help to have time free most afternoons to paint. She continued to paint gods and goddesses in ways that challenged current understandings. She did not care if others accepted her paintings, but buyers from the city loved them. "It's a changing world," buyers shared with Nani, "and your paintings provide inspiration to seek beauty beyond the known."

Azad remained inspired by the light he saw in the forest foliage, and how the nature spirits and light beings magically blended their light with the light that radiated from within the vegetation. He attempted to capture that magic in his paintings. His paintings were also selling. "I have my own space to paint in, but I often go to Auntie's house to paint, especially when Nani is there," he said one night as we lingered by the fire. "Our shared inspiration creates deeper beauty in our separate paintings. The unfinished painting of your dragon remains on its easel where it was left. We all enjoy its company."

I shared little of my time in the forest but did tell him that my dragon visited me and taught me much. I was not specific with any details, and Azad understood my silence.

Everything felt too sacred to be spoken of. I could share its deep magnificence only in my painting.

Azad also shared stories of Pari and Himmat. He recognized Himmat's discomfort with him when he first stayed at the house. He gave Himmat much space but found opportunities to share humor with him. Slowly, Himmat warmed to him, although Azad was careful to always give him space. He also told me of Himmat's marriage six months ago. His wife was much like Himmat in her comfort level with him.

Pari reminded him so much of Mother. Azad experienced her as kind and accepting of him. He understood her limitations in being able to fully understand his ways, but their differences never impacted her acceptance of him. "There are surprises about your siblings waiting for you when you return. It's not my place to tell you about them."

After four weeks of traveling, I knew we were getting close to the bus stop. My body froze, as fear returned to it. Azad read my fear. "In a couple of days, we will be at the bus stop. It will be awkward initially, but I assure you that many things have changed in your village. Nani and Auntie know of your return and have spoken to your family to help them prepare as well."

Azad attempted to humor me because he saw fear creep in. To some degree, he did help to keep my fear from escalating. But we both knew that only I was responsible for what fear I allowed and did not allow. If I chose to make my mind my master, I became its fear. On occasion, fear prevailed, almost paralyzing me in my tracks. As the heaviness of my worries began to fill space within me, the Earth's surface also contracted into an unyielding density. I was no longer in a space that could allow its support. Each step took effort.

We made a fire the night before we would leave the forest, and I welcomed its warm glow. The glow within Azad's gentle eyes and face provided me with even greater warmth. I felt an affection for him that blossomed over these past four weeks. I was going to talk to him about my affection but was too burdened with fear of my return to do so. Azad looked tired and fell asleep quickly as the flames of the fire began to diminish. I remained by it, too restless to sleep.

Watching the flames playfully dance as they mellowed, they suddenly intensified. From within them, the figure of my dragon emerged. "Aditi," it called to me firmly as waves of colorful light from its voice enveloped me. "Are you allowing the fearless magnificence of your soul's spirit to be who You are, or are you allowing your mind to believe that only it and its fear are real? Choose wisely. Fear is never your Truth." My dragon's form then merged back within the fire's flame and disappeared. Its magnificence, however, continued to envelope me as I breathed it deeply within my beingness. The heaviness of my emotions succumbed to the lightness of my dragon's wisdom. It would be with me for the remainder of my journey home.

It was an early Sunday morning when we approached the bus stop, and the noise and activity of the commuters were home with them. The ride gave me needed time to readjust to being out of the forest. When we got to my village, I covered my face with a hat to avoid being noticed. People were used to Azad bringing an occasional buyer into the village and assumed I was one of them. I was taller and thinner. No one would recognize me walking through the village. We went straight to Auntie's house where she and Nani were cleaning up from their meal. They welcomed me as they always did, making me feel as if I was never away. We embraced each other with loving hugs as tears fell from our eyes.

Auntie immediately showed me to my room. It was a small room with little furniture, but its many windows made its light-filled space feel unlimited. "Simple elegance, just like Auntie and Nani," I thought to myself. They knew exactly what I needed. Auntie said my mother made outfits she thought I would enjoy. Mother kept them simple and comfortable, yet also colorful enough to avoid reminding me of the robes I wore in the forest. I washed and put on some clothes from my closet. There was a cup of chai by my bed. I slowly sipped it, letting the love infused in it nurture my tired body. When every drop was accounted for, I put my head on my soft pillow and fell into a deep sleep.

I awoke early in the morning with the smell of chai spices simmering. I found Auntie in the kitchen preparing breakfast. Assuring me no help was needed, she invited me to take a shower as she finished. I gladly accepted her invitation to do so. Now rested, I could enjoy the hot water falling on my body. I imagined it as a beautiful waterfall of light descending from my dragon's wings. I welcomed back the simple comforts of my great castle. Its magic was even more vibrant than I remembered it to be.

I heard Nani arrive as I dressed. We soon joined each other at the table where Auntie's lamp glowed with the sun's radiance. We each savored the meal in our own way, talking little. Nani and Auntie knew from my eyes what was necessary to know. I was away for only two years, but those two years were potent years of growth. The forest became my teacher when I was away. Having allowed so much of its intuition to blend with my beingness, I was becoming my own teacher. Nani and Auntie could better communicate to me through their heart's telepathic wisdom, gently coaxing me to be present with them through that space.

While I observed some changes in Nani before leaving for the forest, they were much more evident now. Her spirit that twinkled in her eyes was as playful as ever, but her physical strength was not what it once was. She moved her body more slowly, accentuating the depth of grace it embodied. She reminded me of how eloquently my dragon moved its body.

Auntie's face radiated a relaxed joy. The sewing she once did for my father demanded much of her. She always faced deadlines and did not want to sacrifice quality to meet them. She was free of that burden now. Auntie shared her happiness that I was staying with her. "We prepared the room to make it comfortable for you, but you're free to change things as you like."

"I love it Auntie. If changes are made, they will be small."

Nani told me that my parents were anxious to see me. They would like to have dinner with me when they returned from work. She shared some of my parents' initial reaction to my leave. Father expressed the anger she anticipated from him at breakfast. "Your mother and I witnessed the stress your father had experienced from the situation with Auntie's dance, and his attempts to control the reactions of others. I suggested we talk to your father that night about his anger, and the harm that could come to the family and business if he chose to give it power. His anger tempered little during the day, and I was unsure if there would be a willingness on his part to listen."

Nani went on to describe how she and Mother carefully spoke, using the teachings of the temple to encourage my father to listen. They reminded him of his wish to protect the family and business, not bring them harm. He knew that anger created only conflict and suffering. If he could not quell his anger, at least he could pretend it was tamed. Mother asked that for the sake of all, he at least pretend he was not angry.

"Most times, your father did follow our suggestion. Two weeks later, your father surprised your mother and I with observations about his anger. He said that when he was angry, there were many more questions about where you were. When he was pleasant and happy, others seemed much less concerned about things that were bothering him and did not ask about your whereabouts.

"These past two years, I've seen many changes in your father. He continues to push his limits with his shop work, but he is much better at leaving those pressures at work. He relaxes more at home, often sharing laughs with us. You'll find it much easier to talk with him."

Nani, Auntie, and Azad joined me at dinner that night. Himmat and his new wife also lived with Mother and Father. They were not at dinner because Father asked them to substitute for him and Mother at a temple gathering that evening. While Azad shared that Himmat was married for six months, he did not share Mother's news that his wife was three months pregnant. Himmat and his wife wanted many children and were thrilled.

At dinner, we shared only joyful times of the past two years. I spoke about Zaya and our time together. Father asked questions about Zaya's recovering strength, and the type of animals he could hunt as he recovered. He asked if I was ever concerned about my safety with Zaya and other animals of the forest.

"Father," I said with words he would find acceptable. "I came to understand that fear only calls to me things that could harm me. I am not yet completely free of fear, but I am aware when it is present. I breathe compassion within me, while accepting fear's presence. Most times, I am able to find a space of peace."

I saw Father understood my words. "I believe I could benefit from doing the same. I will practice what you shared."

His relaxed smile broke into a small chuckle, and we laughed with him. The gentle tone that spoke through his words assured me he was no longer angry. He understood my allegiance was to my own heart, and not to his ways. He attempted to accept my ways, even though he could not understand them. I could now be with Father because he set free those energies that wanted to control and domesticate my heart. Setting me free from his will was an act of his love for me. I did not know if he recognized how loving his action was to himself as well. The changes I witnessed in him told me that at some level, this love deeply touched and lived within him

While deep changes were evident, this time of reunification with my family and village life was tender. There were challenges ahead with my family as we found our way with each other. The energies of the village felt harsh and unwelcoming compared to the energies of the forest. The light beings at Auntie's house, as well as the presence of Auntie and Nani, soothed my emotions as they arose. My friendship with Azad bloomed within the gentle support he offered me. I did have days when I felt heavy, and I wanted to return to the forest without delay. But each day, I was better able to find the strength not to fall victim to my panic.

Nineteen

Father planned a family gathering in two weeks. Himmat was with his wife when I ran into them on the property before the gathering. He grew into a man, and I barely recognized him. We shared a quick hug, each of us commenting on how the other had grown. He introduced his wife. Although in her early stages of pregnancy, the glow of motherhood was present in her face. Her warmth was evident, but I felt her discomfort with me, as well as Himmat's discomfort. I told them I was in the middle of helping Auntie and needed to return, but I looked forward to the gathering where we could talk more. We shared unspoken relief to go our separate ways.

On the day of the gathering, my mind teased me with nervousness, but I chose to invite my dragon's majesty to ease my discomfort. The gathering did go well. Nani stayed with me for a short time when we first went to the house, easing my discomfort with her playful spirit. In time, she was gone from my side.

Pari and I found a space to be alone together. I noticed how Pari's body had changed when I first saw her. She was eight months pregnant, and her nurturing spirit beamed through her eyes. Her serenity told me she was deeply bonded with her child. "Pari, how beautiful you look carrying your child. You are wearing the peace that motherhood is already gifting to you." As Pari spoke of her married life, her contentment was evident. She, Himmat, and I were born from the same biological parents, but what we needed to feel peace was very different.

She did not ask questions about my choices, and how I spent my time. Rather, Pari expressed her happiness that I returned. "You always made your own choices about what was important. Long ago, I learned to accept and love you just as you are. I am glad you are home. I don't need to concern myself with your safety now. You are thin, but I see a peace in you that you lost before you left. When Nani sensed my worry about you, she assured me that you were well, and I trusted her. Perhaps someday I will better understand the ways of you, Nani, and Auntie, but not understanding them does not change my affection for all of you. Even Azad has won my friendship through his warmth."

Himmat and his wife stayed a comfortable distance after we shared a small, rather awkward conversation. How we knew life and chose to create within it differed vastly. We would stay cordial to one another, but never break our silent agreement not to intrude on the comfort level of the other. Father and Mother were relaxed and cheerful. They wanted the day to go well, and it did. But I was grateful when I could return to Auntie's house as the sun set.

On the second day of my return, I had seen my dragon painting on my easel right where I left it. I believed my dragon experienced the same joy I did when I returned to it. My dragon guided my strokes and choices of color differently than before I lived in the forest. It wanted a lotus in its navel area with a translucent light at its center. I made endless attempts to find the best blends of paint that distinguished the light of creation that dances with the dark, from the translucent light that transcends creation's duality. I finally suggested we paint other parts of itself and return to this experimenting another time. My dragon carried an intensity that cut through anything that might taint its beauty, and it could exhaust me.

I also began a painting of Zaya. Taking a break from painting my dragon was also taking a break from its highly focused and concentrated intensity. What Zaya taught me about fear weaved itself ever so deeply within me as I painted his form. Zaya was Lord Shiva with his courage and bravery to protect creation's light from the deepest forces of its dark. He was the many ascetics I met, and continued to meet, who were willing to make any sacrifice to control the forces of the dark that obstructed the light. But unlike Lord Shiva and the ascetics, Zaya was without the means to engage in the ultimate act of courage. He could not acknowledge his fear to embrace it through grace.

As I painted Zaya, I sensed the weight of his fear. The heaviness his fear carried reflected my own heavy shadow of fear. His presence had helped me release the need to engage in any battle with duality through compassionate acceptance of all, just as it was. Zaya had taught me well, and I wanted the translucent light of grace to be present within his eyes. But I was yet to embrace Auntie's Mastery to paint his eyes with her clarity, just as I could not find the right blend of colors to represent the light of grace in my dragon.

My changing relationship with Nani and Auntie reflected my maturity, and their aging. My relationship with Azad was also changing from being just a friendship. I visited more frequently to share evenings alone. His physical touch communicated a gentle love that aroused and enticed my body's fire of desire. Azad was centered in his heart, and my communication with him through my own heart center flowed with ease. Our separate identities were creating a blended love with its own life essence that we danced together within. There were times when our emotions showed themselves and tested us. But we trusted ourselves, and each other, to act responsibly as we slowly surrendered to our sovereign Intuitive Self, who did not recognize forces that fueled emotions as real.

One day when Azad was not with us as we shared chai, I saw playful twinkles in Nani's eyes dancing. "We see sparks of love between you and Azad," she said as her eyes playfully danced. Nothing more was said. Auntie sat quietly enjoying her chai as she always did, although the slightest grin surfaced on her face.

"You are correct, Nani. We will soon announce our

intentions for marriage. Did you know when I first met Azad that we would get married?"

"I saw the potential for marriage, but other potentials existed as well. You could have married according to your father's wishes. I saw little fulfillment in that path. The deepest purpose of your life, to integrate your sacred essence, would not receive the commitment and attention it needed. But it was not my choice to make. There were a couple of ascetics that could have come into your life when you were in the forest. It was not meant to be for any of you because you were not drawn into the same space, at the same time, to meet. I was also unsure if Azad would choose to return to medical school."

"Do you know where you will be living once married?" Auntie asked.

"Yes. Once married, I will live with Azad as we build another home on this land. Father told me there is plenty of land if I choose to build a home for myself someday. I suspect he and Mother know Azad and I will soon be married."

"You are welcome to stay as long as you need. I enjoyed your time here."

Soon after this conversation, Azad and I announced our anticipated engagement. When others complimented Father on the choice of husband that they assumed he made, he politely thanked them. The construction of our new home began.

A couple of months after my return, I found the strength to face the villagers by going into town with Auntie as she did her errands. If someone asked about my absence, I replied, "All of my creations are well and always were well, even when I was absent from the village." A bit perplexed, they usually nodded and excused themselves. Most times, Auntie was within my vicinity. Her grace greatly assisted to ease any need for further probing. The potential to stir village gossip about me died out quickly. After a month of being with Auntie, I wandered through the village alone without attention coming to me.

Azad's father knew of his success as a painter. The success of his son returned to him the respect he desired from others. Azad seldom had contact with his parents. He knew they were relieved he did not live nearby, even though they never expressed their preference verbally. His uncle was aging, but he continued to paint and sculpt. Azad made buyers aware of his uncle's art, which was also rewarded with good money. His money was given to Azad's father for the store. His uncle's back room housed the energies of his inspiration, and he made no changes. However, the store was now owned by his own merit.

A little over six months passed since my return, and preparations were underway at the temple to celebrate a holiday. Last year, Azad went to the temple, along with my family, to celebrate. Azad told me of the fun they had. I saw no reason why I should not go with them. I no longer carried the fear I once held about losing control in light. I matured into a growing clarity that this light represented my soul's spirit. I trusted Its grace enough to dance playfully with Its light whenever I allowed this dance. It could never be tainted by emotions that could not touch It. Only my human mind would know suffering by choosing to let its emotions rule.

The light energy of the priest weaved itself within the physical structure of the temple and the hearts of his congregation. Closing my eyes to breathe the energy of the temple deep within, I felt the eagle's presence. The temple walls became porous and spacious as their solid structure was transformed into the wings of an eagle. The blazing light of its wings blanketed all of space, inviting those present to be touched by it. I accepted its invitation as my breath unified with the eagle's expanded breath of light. I knew that this simple, humble priest was a Master of true magic.

People allowed what was inconceivable before his arrival. Even Nani's painting of Kali was placed quite close to her fearful statue. Looking closely at her painting, the eyes of goddess Kali spoke to me of change. "Be patient," her eyes said to my heart. "Always find your strength in compassion for yourself. Nurture yourself through the breath of your soul's spirit."

Shortly after my return from the forest, I was told that Nani, and a handful of men and women, met each month in secrecy at the home of a neighbor on the outer edge of the village after Auntie's temple dance. Those who met were touched deeply by the beauty of Auntie's dance and could not negate it. They feared the harmful effects of gossip to speak honestly of their beliefs in public, but they wanted to understand what moved them so deeply that night.

The group grew to 10 people who no longer met secretly. The minds of those attending were deeply conditioned with the beliefs and values of our culture. Their doubts and fears continually created confusion and resistance. Like all journeys into the depths of creation's light and dark, the dark within the roots of their lotus emerged that needed acceptance to be transmuted. There were times when people left the group for a while, but all had returned to continue their work.

Auntie and Nani laid a foundation for me to draw strength and Truth from, and Azad's uncle did the same for him. The magic of our spirit's intuition breathed Its essence within the cells of our mind and body into our adolescent years. The intuition the others knew during their toddler years was denied as Truth by their developing identities as young children. Cracks were present within their identity to be touched by Kali's light during Auntie's dance. However, it would take much time for the breath of their spirit to find the space necessary to lift them from the heaviness of their accepted beliefs and charged emotions.

Azad attended the meetings to help Nani and Auntie when I was in the forest and found them helpful. After the temple celebration, I told Nani and Auntie I wanted to attend the meetings as well, which were now held at the temple. For as long as traces of my shadow remained, fear would tease me. Zaya was always present as a reminder of the consequences for choosing to empower fear.

Pari and Mother did not attend the group meetings, but we usually met together every month. Pari brought her child.

Mother joined us when she did not have other business to do. I was aware that Mother sometimes created work to avoid our conversations. Being much older than Pari, her mind was not as flexible to question ingrained beliefs. Mother also buried painful memories related to Auntie's dance and could not open the door to resolve that pain. She preferred to keep herself busy with the business. Pari surprised me with questions about the forest as our comfort level with each other grew. When Mother was with us, she listened with interest, but never asked questions. I shared only what their hearts were ready to hear, just as Nani and Auntie did with me.

The last six months prior to my marriage were busy. I found it challenging to manage the details of building a home, while also staying present in light. Many times, fear suggested limits of what could be afforded. Nani and Auntie witnessed my fear and other emotions arise as various decisions were made. "Remember," Auntie said through eyes that I continued to melt into, "the space you choose to create from will determine the beauty of your creations." I had days when I would give anything to be ignorant of a beauty I did not want diminished by fear.

We always found time to have chai together, often sharing stories of our lives during the time we were apart. One day, Auntie showed me a sketch of the village I visited in the forest. The woman who served me was also in the sketch. I was amazed at how Auntie captured her elegance.

"How did this woman know so much about me?"

"She lived in that village for many years. She was at least 20 years younger when she left her village to seek freedom and was unable to return to it. It is her joy to serve those on their inner journey. When I separated from you and Nani during our last trip together in the forest, I took supplies to her, including the shawl she gave you. For many years, I have taken supplies to her. Nani was quite sure you would venture there and packed special supplies for you, including the shawl."

Twenty

I was up early witnessing a magnificent golden sunrise. Its rays warmed the cool, crisp air and blessed the Earth as they gently lengthened themselves to greet it. I believed I saw my dragon's form within the sun, and its wings outlined in the sun's rays that touched the Earth. Perhaps its appearance was its gift to me on my wedding day.

The wedding and reception were at the home of my parents. Only our immediate families attended our simple, but elegant wedding. Azad's family, including his uncle, traveled to our village to celebrate the day. They arrived the night before. Azad's parents stayed with my parents, and his uncle stayed with Azad. It was the first time I met his uncle, and I recognized the wisdom he embodied. He was a gift to Azad, just as Nani and Auntie were a gift to me. I also felt the hardened and aloof energy of his parents. Their constricted emotions were a concrete wall that could not enable the inner beauty of their divine hearts to touch them. However, I recognized their effort to warm to our wedding celebration.

The temple priest resided over our vows, accepting the words Azad and I created to represent our union. Father did not show his discomfort about many details of our wedding, but I recognized its presence. His willingness to override his discomfort was evident in the affectionate toast he gave to our union. Father's gesture of acceptance was the greatest wedding gift I received from him. Mother and Pari looked like royal queens. It was their way of expressing their love. Their beauty glowed even more as they aged. Even Himmat requested that I dance with him a handful of times, while joyfully celebrating as we danced. It was perfect in every way.

Our own house was completed two months later. We shared the relief that the ongoing decision-making related to its construction was behind us. We were making Azad's house into an art studio. Three months after we moved in, I was pregnant. In the five years that followed, we had two more children. They were young now, and we saw only tendencies in the destiny each would follow. We arranged a separate room in the art studio with supplies for crafts, writing, and painting for the children to create as they wished.

We gave our children their freedom to follow their own paths at birth. We would not force our ways on them. This may not be the lifetime they chose for their inner lotus to fully bloom. They would receive from us what they were able to receive. We could encourage their curiosity and imagination, but it was not our place to tamper with the responsibility that belonged to them. As Nani and Auntie set me free, Azad and I must stay true to our commitment to set our own children free. I now understood the strength for such love was sourced from grace. It was a strength barren of force that needed to control others, including our children.

Each year, Nani's body grew a little weaker. She loved being with the children and painted less. Her time with them gave me more time to paint, although I preferred to join Nani and the children. Nani's playful grace nurtured them in much the same way she nurtured me. Her actions revealed that true nurturance was the infusion of grace into the simplest acts of doing. "Thank you, Nani," I whispered to her as I watched her with the children, "for making me aware of the potency that can be present in simple acts of doing through grace." I knew she received the gratitude my words held.

The paintings of my dragon and Zaya were as complete as I could make them. Although some buyers were interested in buying them, I could not part with them. They hung in honored places in the children's bedrooms. My dragon briefly appeared on occasion to remind me of my Truth when I empowered my emotions. My devotion to my soul's spirit, and my commitment to Its realization, deepened every time my dragon appeared. Its appearances were brief, but potent. My dragon gave up on its need to perfect the translucent light it sought in its painting. It understood I had yet to fully embrace this light. Until that time, the dark would always tease my creations with its presence.

Azad needed to be with his painting much more than me. When he painted, the nature spirits and light beings reminded him of his Truth. Lately, the changes in the Earth during the monsoon season begged his attention. His paintings were increasingly reflecting the blending of the light and dark within the forest foliage, creating a grandeur that teased the transcendence of both. He was allowing light to spiral ever more deeply into the depths grace offered, while compassionately accepting any darkness that showed itself to him.

Now freed of the burden of sewing, Auntie's passion expanded into bottomless depths. The clarity in the eyes of the animals she painted communicated a compassion that knew no limits to its existence. The same was true for Auntie's translucent eyes. They were the eyes of the goddess Kali who fully tamed the lion by transcending the force of creation's duality. They were the light beam at the center of the lotus that my dragon's form outwardly appeared from, and inwardly disappeared into. My dragon's act of appearance and disappearance was an illusion of its Mastery. Its Truth was the translucent light beam at its center whose formlessness remained unchanged, despite any change in the physical form it assumed.

The paintings of Nani and Auntie held the magic of true Master magicians. Their essence was weaved into their art, inviting souls sensitive to their magical energy to awaken. Perhaps it was because I was not yet that magician that I was less inclined to paint. My time would come to embrace painting once again.

Pari now visited our home a couple of times each month. She had two more children. The children played well together as Pari and I enjoyed each other's company. For Pari, our time together was a needed break from the increased responsibilities of her household. The health of her husband's mother was failing. Her husband's sister left to be married. More help was recently hired, but Pari spent much time assisting to teach them how things needed to be done. It was Pari's nature to be content, but I saw fatigue in her. Perhaps it was her need not to allow discontentment to enter her life that led her to always ask questions about the forest. I remained careful not to challenge her beliefs beyond what her mind could tolerate.

Mother's interest in the shop, and new designs for clothing, occupied most of her time. She loved to see others in the village wearing the clothing she designed. At some point, she stopped her visits with Pari and me. We shared an unspoken respect for our different ways. Azad and I sometimes shared dinner with Mother and Father. Nani and Auntie were usually there as well, but sometimes Nani watched the children so we could eat in peace. The conversations were light and conducive to all. I felt a growing ease with Father that surprised me. The sharp edges to his beliefs were melting into a deeper love for himself. He had changed, just as Nani said, and he continued to expand into this change.

Father's business, and his wish to protect the family as he understood he should, continued to capture his complete attention. Himmat followed in Father's footsteps and was consumed with the business as well. Himmat's wife liked to spend her free time with her own friends and family.

The discomfort I experienced from Himmat and his wife remained, but it lessened to some degree after my wedding day. They were sometimes present at dinners with Father and Mother.

Very recently, Father and Himmat celebrated a good business year with a feast for the employees at the home I once lived in. We all participated in preparing food and serving them. When everything was cleaned up, Mother and Himmat's wife left to do errands. Azad returned to our house to relieve Nani of the kids. I lingered behind to enjoy one more cup of chai in the peace that followed. Father knew I was still in the house, but Himmat thought I left.

Himmat began to voice concerns about his oldest son who loved visiting Auntie to talk and paint. Although his son was only six years old, he was very inquisitive and wise for his age. Sometimes he wandered into our art studio, creating works that revealed the depths of the old, wise soul he embodied. "I'm concerned about what he is learning when at Auntie's and the studio. I love Auntie and Aditi, but I do not wish my children to grow into their ways. What can be done to discourage the visits, Father, without hurting anyone?"

Father was silent for a while. When he began to reply, his voice carried a compassion I never heard before. "My dear son. How deeply I love you. And it is because of my love for you, and for those you speak of, that I give you this advice. Let your children decide their own destiny. I was so self-righteous in my belief of what was right for Aditi that I almost destroyed any true contentment she could know in her life. I do not understand the ways of your sister, Azad, Auntie, and Nani, but I have learned to love them despite their ways. In fact, I am grateful for how Nani and Auntie taught Aditi.

"You and I worry about business all the time. I seldom see worry on their faces. When money gets a little low, a buyer shows and usually offers more than what they anticipated receiving. A magical rhythm appears present in their work, and the gratuities they receive from it."

"But Father," Himmat objected, "my son will be ridiculed by others. He does not understand the adult world. Shouldn't I protect his interests? Look at the humiliation that came to Auntie Kiara and Aditi. I want to spare him such hardships."

"I believe their hardships were caused, at least in part, by denying them the freedom to be who they needed to be. I am not suggesting you can protect your son from all the hardships that may or may not come to him from the choices he makes as he matures. But I believe he will learn his own ways of protection, just as I have seen those you speak of do. He has very wise women supporting him.

"They all mingle among others with ease when necessary. They respect the ways of others, but do not care what others think of them. They do not allow themselves to be coerced into making the beliefs and fears of others become their beliefs and fears. Love your son for who he is. Give him the freedom to explore and evolve as he wishes. Do not force your ways on him. You have two other sons to inherit your business. Although very young, they seem inclined to this work. It is your choice Himmat, but you asked for my advice."

Himmat was silent as they got up to return to work. When my brother was out of sight, I shared a smile with Father. He said those words not only for Himmat, but for me as well. "Father's dragon aroused his curiosity when I thought it was benign. No wonder I am seeing so much change in him. Perhaps when he begins to phase out of his business responsibilities, he will begin to question his deeply ingrained beliefs," I thought with a grin.

I floated home to share my joy of Father's words with Azad. My joy was not that Father accepted me. I was accepting all that I am, including my shadow, and did not seek acceptance from anyone to define my worth. The joy I felt was being a witness to the arousal of Father's inner heart. As the days passed, the visits of Himmat's son to Auntie's house continued with the same frequency.

Twenty-One

Auntie, Azad, and I went into the forest twice each year since my return. We needed its nurturance and inspiration, which our two-week visits provided us. Unable to join us, Nani watched the children at home. Azad made two additional trips into the forest each year by himself. On one visit, he met the village woman who helped me years ago with supplies for the ascetics. On his other solo trip through the forest, he traveled to visit his uncle. The deepening light and dark of the forest continued to enrich him, and the paintings he infused his energy in.

Although Nani's body was not with us when the three of us ventured into the forest together, she always made her presence known. We had a guessing game about what form she would assume each time we entered the forest. The first time in the forest after my return, we were guided to the cliff where I first blended my awareness with the eagle. We recognized Nani's presence in the body of an eagle, joyfully circling us. The eagle, free of Zaya's fear, soared gracefully above all else in the sky. But it could not teach me about my shadow as Zaya had.

When we returned from our first trip into the forest, Auntie asked if I still had the painting that she gifted me when I was in the forest alone. Asking no questions, I gave it to her. Almost a month later, I found the painting on my easel next to the painting of Zaya. Auntie repainted the eagle's wings and my eyes. The dark clouds that shadowed the wings of the eagle disappeared. Its wings now opened boldly to reveal a radiance that lit up the sky. My once vacant eyes were now ablaze with the translucent light of my dragon's wings. It was the shade I made endless attempts to create in my dragon painting. I told my dragon to be patient as I evolved into the Mastery necessary to represent this light with Auntie's stunning accuracy.

On occasion, Azad and I brought our children into the forest for a couple of nights. I sometimes heard the soft moan of Zaya. While his moan was welcoming the children, it still carried the fear that created his need to protect them. Engaging in the action of protection was what male lions did. He remained my protector, even though I did not need his protection. He sensed my unwillingness to live in harmony with his ways, but he was without the means to understand why.

Nani's physical strength waned quite quickly in the last couple of years, and she used a cane to support her body. I sensed she was making the choice to soon leave her body.

One day, Azad offered to stay at home with the children so I could enjoy chai with Nani and Auntie without interruption. Nani spoke of leaving us. She said her soul enjoyed what the Earth shared with her, but the time would soon come to leave her body behind. "Never mourn the loss of my bodily presence, Aditi," she told me with her eyes dancing in their joy. "You know true magicians can be present in whatever way they wish, whether they have a body or not."

As Nani spoke, she took her cane that rested on the table into her hand. Her body and cane began to glow with increasing intensity. When she stopped speaking, she stood. Her bodily form became so luminous that it was of light vibrations only. A magnificent dragon appeared from within this light. Its eyes twinkled with the magic of Nani's eyes. Nani's cane became a wand that floated in the dragon's hand as a very slight movement.

"Aditi," its strong, joyful voice bellowed, "please stand." A crown of twinkling stars drifted from its wand, over my head, and down to my feet covering me in a blanket of eloquent stars. The joy that enveloped me set free any concerns I had of Nani's leaving. I was given time to experience this dragon's radiant joy, although I was not yet ready to embody the totality of its expansiveness.

Words from the dragon that spoke to my heart, while silent to my outer ears, continued to flow from its quasi-physical body. "No need for concern about Nani. Her soul will visit you often in the many forms It can assume. You are so close to the full realization of your Truth. I know you will not leave this Earth before doing so. You have gifted all of creation with the choices you made."

The form of the dragon dissipated as Nani's body and cane slowly lost their glow, while solidifying into physical form once again. Nani sat and rested her cane that now required the support of the table. I also sat, grateful for a chair to support the lightness of my body. Slowly, my blanket of stars dissipated, but its joyful presence would be with me forever.

We were all silent as we sipped the remains of our chai. When Nani finished what was left of her chai, she looked at me. "I always cherish the presence of the dragon," her joyful voice shared. She then stood, steadied her body with her cane, and left to return to the house I once shared with her.

It was just another day in the magical world of Nani and Auntie. They were true magicians. Having transcended all of creation's polarities of the light and dark to Exist as multi-dimensional beings, they never confused the difference between illusion and Truth.

Azad and the children were out playing one day so I could clean the children's bedroom where my dragon's painting hung. While wishing for its presence as I delicately dusted its wings, my dragon's voice answered me. "Aditi," my dragon said as my heart received the vibrations of its voice. I sat on the bed, breathing deeply into my heart to receive the vibrations of light my dragon wished to share. "You have prepared well for this moment. It is now time to embody your deepest Truth. Please stand and allow me to support your body."

Now fully centered within the vision of my divine heart, I witnessed the vibrations of my dragon's painting swirling outward toward me. My dragon's form appeared in front of me. Its compassionate eyes pierced my inner depths. Lifting its magnificent wings, it effortlessly separated its form into an eagle and a serpent. The eagle flew to a space above my head and hovered over it, while glowing a brilliant light. The serpent brought its entire body to the floor. It radiated a sublime, translucent light. Creation's synchronistic movements of its opposing clockwise and counterclockwise spirals flowed within its form.

Mesmerized by the flow of the spirals, I was pulled into them, while simultaneously blending with them. My body lost its sense of balance and placement on the floor, and I sensed I was falling. I felt the support of my dragon as a gentle strength that touched my body. Relaxing into my dragon's quiet strength, my attention was guided back to the serpent. For the first time, I embodied the totality of creation's dual movement that the serpent embodied, and I became it. All noise from my thoughts and emotions dissipated within a silence that held only the most sacred vibrations of creation's energy. Its polarized forces existed only as potentials. The inbreath of my heart supported the outbreath of my mind.

I felt a very slight movement as I gracefully divided my serpent form into identical twin serpents. A pang of fear showed itself, wanting to escalate its presence. "Stay present in the purity of these vibrations," my dragon said to my heart. "Remember, fear is an illusion. Your Truth can create any form, while remaining as the unchanging grace of your

Intuitive Self and Eternal Self. The serpent embodies the grace that You are as your deepest Truth. Do not be teased by emotions that want to surface within your human mind. If you allow fear, you will not be able to realize the magic this moment holds for you."

Breathing ever deeper into this grace, I allowed it to aid the fear wanting attention. My inbreath now calmed the turbulence that teased me with fear, and my outbreath released fear's energy. Freed of distraction, my attention was guided back to the serpents. As one serpent, I effortlessly glided toward the feet of my human body. As the other serpent, I gracefully lifted my form to ascend. I stopped at a space over my head, slightly below where the eagle rested.

Sharing the essence of the two serpents, I felt a slight movement as each serpent divided its form to create another twin, a moment prior to entering my body. Moving within creation's most sacred vibrations, the two serpents glided upward from my feet. In synchrony with them, the other two serpents glided downward from my head. I experienced each cell lovingly ingested, cleansing any remaining darkness. The eagle's searing light filled the vacant chambers within the cells of my human mind and body.

Meeting at my navel area, the four serpents intertwined, merging as the original serpent. All movement ceased. The wings of the eagle fully expanded as it reunited with the serpent to assume my dragon's form. The bliss I knew felt explosive as my dragon dissipated into a space of white light, deep within my navel area. I became present in my human body as a quasi-physical form, full of light. I initially thought

I had died, but then saw that my physical body was still present and standing.

Gaining a bit of focus, I watched in great awe as a spiral of golden light emerged from within my navel cavity, moving to the front of me. My dragon's brilliant, luminous form appeared from within it. In its hands was a lotus. As my dragon opened each lotus petal, the light flowing to me intensified. Breathing this light through the hollow bones of my body, my breath unified with my spirit's breath. When all petals were fully extended, a translucent light emerged from within the center of the lotus that tenderly massaged what was now my light body.

The carbon-based biological structure that once defined me was fully transmuted to support the crystalline-based light body of my soul that fully descended into my beingness. I realized the Master magician within. My beingness was no longer my human self alone. I Existed as the sacred triangle that is my human self, my Intuitive Self, and my Eternal Self, all unified within the grace of Consciousness. "I Am" a multi-dimensional being. I befriended the translucent light beam of my dragon's inner lotus, and I was set free.

About the Author

B etsey Grobecker has had a life-long yearning to know a deeper truth to her existence that could not be found in the teachings of western science and Catholicism of her heritage. Leaving her cultural truths behind, Betsey explored Native American Shamanism, Peruvian Shamanism, Indian Vedanta, and New Energy Consciousness, while working closely with spiritual Masters of these traditions. Her passion is to share her insights of the perilous mythic journey within, where all is risked, to follow the calling of the divine heart and realize true magic.

www.ingramcontent.com/pod-product-compliance
Lightning Source LLC
Chambersburg PA
CBHW032002240626
47153CB00003B/1085